# Will she say *Yes*, just this once?

As a minister's daughter, Shannon Walsh was raised to say *No* to a lot of temptations, with the male of the species at the top of that list. She's an adult now, making her own choices, but until Mr. Right comes along she plans to keep resisting the call of the wild.

Then Rick Hardison moves in next door. The handsome rascal doesn't appear to have spent many hours inside a church, and he doesn't waste any time drawing Shannon inside his wickedly sexy arms. What's a good girl to do when the man of her dreams is a very bad boy?

———

"*Just This Once* is a must-read for lovers of well-written, sensual contemporary romance."
—Connie Ramsdell, *Bookbug on the Web*

# Trish Jensen Novels
# From Bell Bridge Books

The Harder They Fall

Stuck With You

Against His Will

Just This Once

Nothing But Trouble

For A Good Time, Call

Phi Beta Bimbo

# Just This Once

by

# Trish Jensen

Bell Bridge Books

This is a work of fiction. Names, characters, places and incidents are either the products of the author's imagination or are used fictitiously. Any resemblance to actual persons (living or dead), events or locations is entirely coincidental.

Bell Bridge Books
PO BOX 300921
Memphis, TN 38130
Print ISBN: 978-1-61194-294-1

Bell Bridge Books is an Imprint of BelleBooks, Inc.

A mass market edition of this book was published by Kensington Publishing Corp/ Precious Gems #162 in 1998

We at BelleBooks enjoy hearing from readers.
Visit our websites – www.BelleBooks.com and www.BellBridgeBooks.com.

10 9 8 7 6 5 4 3 2 1

Cover design: Debra Dixon
Interior design: Hank Smith
Photo credits:
Badge (manipulated) © Keith Bruce | Dreamstime.com
Photo (manipulated) © Curaphotography | Dreamstime.com

:Ltjo:01:

# Dedication

To my awesome nephews, Wren Graves, and Peter Graves Kruchten, who make me so proud, every single day. Talented (because of me), smart, (well, maybe sister) wonderful, (me again) funny (me, me, me) handsome (on your own) young men, who obviously take after their Aunt Trish. Your mother might disagree, but you are my kids, through and through. I've loved watching you grow up to be the men you are. You just grew up way too fast.

# Chapter One

THE DOG WAS going to kill her.

Shannon Walsh stood frozen, staring into the feral amber eyes of a mangy, overgrown, snarling German shepherd. A German shepherd who'd somehow managed to invade her back yard. Her fenced in back yard.

How had he gotten in? And why? It wasn't like Shannon had committed any crime. She glanced down at the skimpy, damp lingerie she'd come outside to hang dry. Uh-oh.

Was this beast her punishment for buying such wicked underwear? Was it a sign from above that she'd done something unforgivably sinful?

Her father would shout a resounding "yes!" Reverend Felker Walsh would consider owning lacy, sexy underwear as a sign of possession by the devil. She let the bra and panties slip from her fingers.

The dog took a step forward.

"Good doggie," Shannon said faintly.

The dog growled, apparently disagreeing with her.

She took a step back, searching her peripheral vision for any possible weapon. Directly to her left lay a rolled up hose. She had the feeling the menacing animal ten feet in front of her would eat a rubber hose for a snack.

A one hundred and twelve pound woman would make a nice meal.

She backed up again, and this time felt the bite of brick against her shoulder blades. She chanced a quick glance to her right. The porch door that led into her kitchen stood about fifteen interminable feet away. She'd never make it.

She looked back at the beast stalking her. "Where . . . are

you from, big boy?" she asked, then winced. That sounded like a bad pick-up line. "I . . . don't recognize you."

The dog cocked his ears back, then did a quick one-two over his shoulder. That's when Shannon noticed the green collar around his neck. She spotted some kind of stitched writing on it, but with fear clogging her throat and fogging her brain, she couldn't make out the words.

The dog turned back to her and growled.

She took a step sideways, testing his waters.

His waters didn't like being tested. The German Shepherd jumped like a jackrabbit, hung his head low, and snarled at her.

Every nerve in her shook. Spots started bursting in front of her eyes. She was going to die. She'd moved to DC to spice up her life. This was not the sort of spice she'd been looking for.

Tears stung her eyes. She knew she should be praying for salvation, but not a single prayer came to mind. All she could think about were the things she'd never done, the things she'd miss if this dog killed her.

She'd never been to Sea World.

She'd never tried skydiving.

She'd never been to a male strip club.

She'd never had a wild, illicit love affair.

"If I make it out of this alive," she whispered. "I'm going to have a fling."

The dog cocked his head at the sound of her voice. Encouraged, she kept talking. "That's right, a fling. A torrid affair with a man who's all wrong for me."

The dog seemed interested in her fantasy, so Shannon elaborated. "He'll be big and rough and he'll swear like a sailor. He'll be handsome in a roguish sort of way. He'll be . . . a bad boy. One of those men who would make my parents faint if they saw him."

Slowly she raised her arm and passed a shaky hand over her brow. "We'll take one look at each other and know it's inevitable. We'll be so hot for each other we won't even make it to the bedroom."

Keep talking girl. As long as he's listening, his fangs will stay put. "We'll spend one night—just one—making wild, passionate love." Her hand dropped. "And then I'll go home and do what's right."

A small sob forced its way past her lips. The thought of doing what was right left her stone cold. Probably because she'd been doing what was right all her life. Her boring life. Just once, she wanted to do something wrong. Well, not wrong exactly. Just . . . reckless.

Rover or Fido, or more likely Killer, hunkered down and whined. Suddenly, he didn't appear quite so menacing.

Taking a deep breath Shannon shoved off from the wall. The dog jumped, his hind-quarters bunched and, in horror, Shannon watched as he leapt toward her.

In that eternal instant, regret at all she'd miss burned in her soul. She cried out, bracing herself for the agony of torn flesh.

The beast's huge paws collided with her shoulders, slamming her against the house. Her head cracked against the unforgiving brick with a dull thud.

Shannon almost blacked out, but a last shred of survival instinct reared up inside of her, and she shook her head to clear it. That was when she realized that the dog hadn't torn into her jugular at all, but just stood on his back legs, pinning her to the wall.

She looked into its brown eyes and saw . . . concern. No, not possible. Still, the dog's tongue hung out the side of its mouth, and it didn't seem intent on ripping her apart. It just didn't want her to move for some reason.

"Good doggie?" she whispered.

The dog's oversized tongue slurped her cheek. Shannon tentatively patted its side. The slobbering beast loved it.

"Down boy," Shannon said, trying to sound friendly yet commanding.

Amazingly, the dog got down and stood there, wagging its long tail.

Why hadn't she thought of this before? "Sit!" Shannon said.

The dog handed her his paw.

Close enough. "Lie down."

The dog sat.

Bemused, Shannon rubbed the back of her head. "Sit!"

Again, he offered his paw, his tail swishing through the grass in an arc.

Shannon dropped to her knees, and raised a trembling hand to the dog's head. His tongue lolled, and she could swear his mouth lifted in an adoring smile as she gave him scratches.

"You're not a killer at all, are you, you phony?"

The dog tilted his head, leaning into her petting hand.

"Who do you belong to, anyway?" she asked, as she spied the writing on the collar again.

She turned the collar so she could read it. There were the words NO DRAH and an upside down phone number. Shannon's forehead furrowed as she leaned forward and read it right side up. "Oh, my God!"

What kind of jerk would call his dog HARD ON? She knew for certain it had to be a man. No self-respecting woman would be that crude.

"You poor baby!" she cried, indignant on the innocent animal's behalf. She scruffed his thick chest fur. "Do you want to come inside, Har . . . doggie?"

The dog barked. Shannon slowly got to her feet, lest the poor puppy decide to pin her against the house again. "Come on, let's get you a treat. Then I'll call your master and give him a piece of my mind." She sidled along the wall toward the porch. The dog followed. "Maybe I'll even call animal services. That must be cruel and unusual punishment or something."

They reached the porch, one hesitant step at a time. Shannon didn't feel exactly comfortable turning her back on Har . . . the animal, but she didn't have much choice. He literally dogged her steps.

She took a breath, whirled and raced up the four concrete stairs. With a yip, the dog bounded after her, but thankfully didn't tackle her.

She opened the screen door and waved the dog in. As regally as a king, he swept into her house.

Considering she'd only be in Northern Virginia four more

months, Shannon had decided not to get herself a cat, for which, at the moment, she felt eternally grateful. The dog made himself at home, sniffing his way around her modest ranch style house.

Then he returned to the kitchen and looked up at her expectantly. Shannon couldn't bring herself to call the dog Hard On, so she mentally renamed him King.

She didn't have doggie snacks on hand, so she grabbed lunch meat from the fridge. Tearing off some chipped ham, she said, "Speak!"

King dropped to the floor and performed a not-so-graceful one-eighty.

"Lie down!"

King sat.

"Roll over!"

King laid down again and went limp, playing dead. Apparently the jerk who owned him spoke a different language.

Shannon set down a large bowl of water. King managed to get more on the floor than in his mouth.

While he drank, Shannon grabbed the phone and dialed work.

"Lab," the bubbly receptionist answered.

"Hi, Molly, it's Shannon. Can you put me through to Diane?"

After a moment, Shannon's boss and friend answered. "Mackenzie."

"Hi, Diane, it's Shannon."

"Oh, no, don't tell me you're sick!"

"Nope, I'm just running a little late. I got shanghaied in my back yard this morning."

"Oooh, please tell me he was tall and dark and gorgeous!"

"Not exactly," she said, looking at a now resting King. "He's a dog."

"Hey, honey, sometimes the dogs are the best in bed! Go for it."

Shannon rolled her eyes. She'd never met anyone like Diane in her life. The woman could turn a discussion of the results of a phenylthaline test into a discussion of men. "No, I mean he's an honest-to-goodness, woof-woof dog."

"Oh. In that case, get your butt into work. Preston wants results back on the Chambers case today. He needs to know if there's enough here to indict."

"I'll be in as soon as I call the owner and turn this beast over to him."

"How do you know the owner's a him?"

Clucking, Shannon said, "Call it a hunch."

"Well, if the owner's cute, I give you permission to take an extra half hour. You can make up for it tonight."

"Do you ever think about anything besides sex?"

"Not a chance."

Laughing, Shannon hung up. Phone in hand, she bent beside King and turned his collar so the phone number was visible. Then, her indignation growing as she punched in the number, she stood and started pacing. The phone rang five times before she heard the click of a machine.

"Leave your name and number. I'll get back to you."

A shiver raced up Shannon's spine. She pulled the phone from her head and stared at it, wondering if her ears were playing tricks on her. Just a few terse words, growled into the phone, and she went hot and cold all over.

She'd never heard a more dangerous, masculine voice in her life. It was low and rumbly and commanding, and it conjured images of a darkly handsome man, confident, arrogant and supremely, utterly male.

That was a bad boy voice if she'd ever heard one.

Abruptly she realized that several seconds, maybe minutes, had passed since the phone had buzzed at her. Quickly she punched the "off" button, breaking the connection.

Taking several deep breaths, she looked down at the dog. Definitely, the man who owned that voice would have the audacity to name his dog Hard On.

Steeling herself, she punched in the number again. Strangely, she felt something akin to anticipation while she waited for the machine to pick up. When she heard his voice again, Shannon actually quaked inside. Was it possible to fall in lust with a voice?

After the beep, she said, "Umm, yes, my name is, umm, Shannon Walsh and I . . . I believe I have something of yours. If I have the right number, you're the man who owns, uh, Hard On." Shannon's eyes closed and she stifled a groan of pure agony. She couldn't believe she'd just said that. "That is, I believe I've got your dog. He . . . he was in my back yard this morning." She swallowed. "I . . . have to go to work. I'll tie him in the yard so he doesn't run away again. That's about the best I can do."

She hesitated again, debating whether to give the man her address. Quickly she discarded that idea, for some reason a thrill of fear trickling through her. No, she didn't think she wanted the man to know her address.

"You . . . you can call me at work today and we can make . . . arrangements." She gave him her work number, hesitating yet again. "Thank you," she finished primly.

She disconnected and slumped into a kitchen chair, burying her head in her hands. Could she possibly have made a bigger fool of herself? She pictured the man, sitting at a bar with his buddies, sipping beer and relating the story of the woman who'd called him.

Straightening, she stiffened her spine. Well, what did the man expect when he called a poor dog that disgusting name? In fact, she thought she just might tell him exactly what she thought of someone who could be so crude. With self-righteousness bolstering her, she left King snoring on the kitchen floor and marched to the bathroom and the shower.

RICK HARDISON checked the clip in his Sig before driving it home. He glanced at his partner, Tom Fletcher, across the threshold of the back door of the warehouse. Fletch nodded.

Rick inspected their backup, and found everyone in place and ready. He lifted his clenched fist high and mouthed, "Three . . . two . . . " as he ticked off fingers. At "one" he swung toward the door and kicked it sharply, once, twice, before the lock gave way.

He and Fletch quickly entered the building, guns leading the way. They found themselves in a store room of sorts, small but well-organized. From the looks of things, the leader of this bookmaking operation—Lucky Louie, their sources called him—kept his employees well-fed. Industrial size jars and cans, huge sacks of flour and sugar, and row upon row of chocolate chips lined the shelves. For a moment Rick wondered if they had the correct address.

He waved his gun, and on cue the uniformed back-up fanned out behind Fletch and him. Silently, he moved to the door opposite the entrance. Stopping to listen, he heard the jangle of phones, and the low hum of dozens of voices, speaking at once. Sure sounded like a book operation to him.

Again he and Fletch flanked the door. Again he checked their backup, before counting down. And again on "one" he shoved open the door, yelling, "Everyone freeze! Don't move! You are, as they say, busted."

Everyone froze, including Rick. He blinked. Then, as his gaze roamed the room, his jaw grew more and more slack. As officers swarmed in behind them, they all seemed to stop in their tracks, too.

Phones went unanswered, as the fifty or so bookies stared in alarm at the number of uniforms filling the warehouse.

It was a remarkable set-up.

Along the near wall was a huge computer screen, where one of their computer geeks kept the bookmakers up to speed on the odds of ball games, horse races, even the chances of The Dancing With The Stars winner.

Every bookmaker had his or her own desk, with what looked like cushy leather chairs. On each desk was a phone, stacked "in-out" trays, books of chits, a small crystal vase with a single daisy and greens, and a plate of chocolate chip cookies.

Beside nearly every desk sat a walker or a cane.

Rick spared a glance at Fletch. "I think we just busted a bingo hall."

At the same time they lowered their weapons. It didn't seem

right to aim them at people who would need a half-hour head start to make good their escape.

It was a bookmaking operation all right.

Run by a team of senior citizens.

Rick shoved aside his army jacket and jammed his gun into the holster at his ribs. He ran his hands through his hair, tucking it behind his ears. "Spread out," he called behind him.

He ambled to the closest bookie, a man who looked to be in his seventies. Or eighties. Or nineties. It was hard to tell.

The man appeared shocked, his mouth frozen in a perfect O. His fingers shook as he pushed his chits to one side.

"Where can I find Lucky Louie?" Rick asked him.

"Eh?"

Rick leaned closer to his ear. "Lucky Louie," he all but shouted.

The man flinched, but his eyes went straight to a door at the back of the room.

"Thank you," Rick said loudly.

He strode directly to the door, as the uniformed cops took on the task of getting down names of the felons.

Fletch followed, muttering under his breath. Rick thought he said something like, "I knew I should've gone into plumbing and heating."

Without knocking, Rick pushed open the door to the office. He found Lucky Louie trying to escape through the single small window.

And Louie would have nearly made it, too. Except that her support hose had snagged on the sill.

As gently as he could, Rick freed the hose, then grasped Louie around the waist and lifted her back into the office. Louie weighed about ninety pounds, had curly blue-white hair, and flailing arms. She wiggled and squealed indignantly as Rick set her on her feet and turned her around.

"Mrs. Sugarbaker!" Rick said, astounded, as he recognized the head of this illegal operation.

He'd just busted the largest contributor to the Police Benevolent Fund.

"AREN'T YOU going to cuff me?" Louise Sugarbaker asked, as Rick and Fletch started leading her out of the warehouse.

"I don't think that will be necessary," Fletch answered gravely. But the amusement in his eyes was unmistakable as he glanced over the tiny woman's head to Rick. "You'll come along peacefully, right?"

"I suppose," she answered, sniffing. She glanced up at Rick. "You need a haircut, Richard."

"Yes, ma'am."

"And a shave."

"Yes, ma'am."

"And your wardrobe is atrocious."

"Yes, ma'am."

"Why, you could take lessons from Thomas, here."

Rick resisted the urge to roll his eyes. Why had he been saddled with a partner who always looked like he was heading to a photo shoot for GQ?

Fletch smirked at him as they headed for his Range Rover.

Mrs. Sugarbaker stopped in her tracks behind Fletch's car. "Oh, my!" she gasped, then looked up at Fletch with patent disapproval. "Thomas Fletcher, what kind of license plate is that?

Fletch stopped and looked. Then gaped. Then scowled. He turned narrowed eyes on Rick, who was holding onto Mrs. Sugarbaker's elbow with one hand, holding his other up to study his nails.

"Hardison, you sonofa—" Fletch began.

"Watch your language, Thomas."

"It's the least you deserve," Rick said, "after what you did to Bert's collar."

"Bert's a da—darn dog. What's he gonna care?"

"It's a matter of his dignity."

"Besides," Fletch ranted on, "nobody but your friends—of which you have few—would see Bert's collar. How long have I been tooling around town with a license plate that reads 'LECHER?'"

Rick waved. "A couple of days."

Fletch leapt forward and started scrubbing at the white ink that covered the "F." "No wonder those babes honked at me this morning. And here I thought it was my awesome good looks."

"Dream on."

Fletch moved to the ink covering the T. "Will this stuff come off?"

"Eventually."

"Sonofa—"

"Thomas!"

"—Gun!"

Rick laughed and helped Mrs. Sugarbaker into the passenger seat. He winked at her as he helped her buckle her seat belt. "No sense of humor."


RICK WEARILY let himself into his house. On a scale of one-to-ten, the bust this morning at the warehouse had been a definite zero. He tried to remind himself why he'd become a cop in the first place. He was pretty damn certain it wasn't for the glory of taking down four dozen senior citizens.

Passing by his desk he punched the blinking button on his answering machine. Shrugging out of his army jacket, he tossed it on the back of his easy chair.

"Rick, it's Lisa. Call me, love."

He ambled to the back door of the house and threw it open, emitting a sharp whistle.

The machine beeped again. "Hey, Hardison. Basketball game tonight at the Y. Seven o'clock. Be there."

Removing his shoulder holster, he threw his weapon in the desk. When Bert didn't come bounding in the house, he headed back to the door to look out.

"Richard, it's me." Rick groaned at the sound of Mary Anne's voice. "Your alimony payment's late. As usual."

Rick hissed a curse. Like she needed the money. The settlement he'd agreed to just to get the divorce moving had made Mary Anne a millionaire several times over. But still she hounded him once a month like clockwork.

He made a mental note to check with his accountant to see if there was a way to pay her off permanently, just so he didn't have to deal with her. She was a constant reminder of the biggest mistake he'd ever made in his life—trying to become something he was not.

Thoughts of Mary Anne vanished when he gazed out over his yard. Bert was nowhere to be seen. The gate was closed, and there were no holes in the ground to indicate he'd dug his way out.

Which wouldn't have made sense anyway. Bert wasn't a wanderer by nature. He knew who his master was, where his home was, and he faithfully watched over his domain. So Rick didn't believe for a moment that Bert had run away. Which left him with one other conclusion.

Someone had taken his dog.

Rick tried not to panic. He tried to come up with a rational plan of action. He tried not to consider what he'd do to whoever had dognapped Bert. His best friend.

" . . . you're the man who owns a hard on."

He spun back to the machine, certain he couldn't have heard that right. He didn't recognize the woman's voice, but if she was trying a new pick-up line, she certainly sounded doubtful about it.

Striding to the machine, he hit replay. After listening to the message, he grinned his relief. One of these days he should invest in a new collar for Bert after Tom's stupid practical joke.

Bert must have jumped the four foot fence. Why? It was so out of character for his dog, it made Rick uneasy. He hoped this wasn't a new game. He and Bert had only lived in this house a little over a month, but Rick had felt that Bert adjusted to his new big back yard well.

Rick swore. Punching the button, he picked up a pen. He wrote the number down, and grinned a little. Poor woman sounded flustered. He supposed she had good reason.

Scratching his temple with the pen, he looked at the phone number. He recognized it as the one for the crime lab. But he didn't know any Shannon Walsh who worked there. Of course, he'd spent the last several weeks spinning his wheels with this bookmaking ring, so hadn't had much reason to visit the crime lab.

Rick dialed the number and flirted with Molly for a couple of minutes before asking to be put through to Shannon Walsh. She answered almost immediately, her soft voice sounding distracted.

"Ms. Walsh, my name's Rick Hardison. I believe you found my dog."

There was a long, long pause—one he'd call almost startled. He wondered about that. After all, she'd given him the number.

She cleared her throat. "Yes, I, uh, believe I did."

"I'm sorry about the inconvenience. Thanks for watching out for him. When can I come and get him?"

"I should get home around . . . seven, Mr. . . . ."

"Call me Rick. What's your address? I'll go look for him now."

"I prefer to bring him to you," she said in a prim and proper little voice.

He threaded his fingers through his hair. "Lady, I want my dog."

"Mr. Hardison, I didn't ask for him to attack me in my yard. I'm sorry if you don't like it—"

"Wait a minute. He attacked you? Maybe this isn't my dog after all."

"Well, he sort of just trapped me. For some reason, he didn't want me going to my clothes line."

"Did he hurt you?"

"No, not really. It didn't take long to realize he's a creampuff underneath that snarl."

Snarl? Bert? Something was wrong.

"I'll tell you what," the woman continued. "I'll call you as soon as I get home. You can give me your address and I'll bring King to you."

"King?"

Another pregnant pause. "Well, I certainly wasn't going to

call him . . . that other name," she snapped, her voice ringing with disapproval.

Rick swallowed a shout of laughter. She sounded like a first class prude. He could just imagine her reaction when she'd first read Bert's collar. He opened his mouth to tell her Bert's real name, but some perverse streak stopped him. "I see," he said, not even trying to hide his amusement. "All right, we'll do it your way."

"Fine."

That one clipped word said a mouthful. He'd bet she wore her hair back in a face-stretching bun. He'd bet she considered the sex act a crime. In fact, he'd bet she'd never had an orgasm in her life.

"I'll be looking forward to your call," Rick said. He guessed the woman had a right to assume he was a pervert. But, she wouldn't have to call him. By the time she got home, he'd be waiting for her.

He called the station. "Fletch, do me a favor . . . oh, good for Mrs. Sugarbaker . . . listen, I need an address . . ."


RICK SHOVED off from an oak tree when the red Ford Escort pulled into Shannon Walsh's driveway.

Her single car garage door lifted, and she drove right in. He thought he glimpsed a flash of blonde hair before she disappeared inside.

The garage door closed before he got another look at her. Rick waited about a minute, then strolled across the street to her red brick ranch style house. The house whose back yard bordered his. He wondered how she'd take that news.

Somehow, he didn't think she'd be thrilled.

He strolled up the flagstone walkway. Her door was painted the same black as the shutters. She had a welcome mat at the entrance, and automatically, Rick wiped his sneakers.

He rang the bell then shoved his hands deep into his jeans pockets.

Several seconds later he heard the scrape of a chain. The

door cracked open, and all he spied was one blue eye. "Yes?"

"Ms. Walsh?" he said, admiring her eye.

"Yes."

"I'm Rick Hardison. The owner of the dog."

That eye went wide, then swept from the top of his head to the tips of his sneakers. Rick felt suddenly self-conscious. His battered Army jacket and torn, faded jeans didn't exactly inspire confidence. Between that and his long black hair, single earring and five o'clock shadow, he had a feeling that her first thought was to slam the door and call the police. He knew he looked like a thug.

He held up his hands. "I'm civilized, I promise. I just want my dog."

"How'd you find out where I live?"

"You're in the book."

"No, I'm not. I haven't lived here long enough."

Oops. "I have a friend at the phone company."

"I believe that's illegal."

Several caustic remarks came to mind. Rick bit them back. "Look, I was really worried about my dog. I want him back."

Her eyes swept his body one more time. "Do you have some sort of identification?"

Rick resisted the urge to whip out his badge and flash it at her. Instead he dutifully pulled out his wallet. He took out his driver's license, careful not to let any condom packages fall out. If she saw them, she'd probably faint.

Holding the license up, he tried to smile reassuringly. Jeez, knowing what type of female he was dealing with, he probably should have been smart enough to clean up his act a little. But he hadn't been thinking too clearly after only four hours of sleep.

She hesitated a moment. That irritated Rick. He didn't care what people thought of him, but he also didn't like her looking at him like he was some kind of rapist.

"Listen, you don't have to invite me in for tea and cookies. But I want to get my dog, and I'd like you to show me where he trapped you."

She shut the door in his face. He stopped himself from

making a rude gesture. Good thing too. Because he heard the scrape of chain again, then she opened the door completely.

Rick's jaw almost hit the pavement.

Prissy little Shannon Walsh was a knockout.

# Chapter Two

RICK HARDISON was a hoodlum.

Why Shannon had broken world records opening her door to him, she didn't know. She should have slammed home the dead bolt and rushed to the phone to dial 911.

Instead, she stood staring at a pair of the blackest eyes to grace the planet. His hair was even darker than his eyes, pulled back in what she feared was a ponytail. His jaw was shadowed with stubble. He had shoulders that would thrill a linebacker, and a diamond stud earring, winking in the fading, early-evening light.

An earring. God, the man was wearing an earring.

A ponytail. God, the man had hair long enough to pull back in a ponytail.

A hunk. God, the man was a hunk.

Shannon realized she was staring rudely at him, but she couldn't stop herself. She'd never seen a more darkly handsome man in her life. Wickedly handsome. Dangerously handsome.

The threat to her life this morning had nothing on the threat to it at this moment. Absently, she noted the danger. And didn't care.

She blurted the first thing that came into her head. "Briefs or boxers?"

The man blinked those dark eyes. Then his lips lifted in a lazy grin. "I'm flexible. Which do you prefer?"

Shannon wanted the earth to swallow her up. She couldn't believe she'd just asked him that. And how did she respond to his own question? Truthfully, "Actually, I think I'd prefer neither," would work.

She vaguely realized that he was checking her out as closely as she was checking him out. She'd never felt this instant draw before, this burst of carnal awareness. It glittered in his onyx eyes, in the tense set of his stubbled jaw.

She had no idea how long they stood, staring at each other. Time seemed to melt around them. They were trapped in a cocoon of mutual attraction. She knew that as surely as if he'd said, "I want you."

They might have stayed that way forever if Shannon's phone hadn't rung. She tore her gaze from him to stare over at it stupidly.

"Aren't you going to answer that?"

Answer it. That's right. When a phone rings you answer it.

She moved to the phone. "Hello."

"Shannon, it's your mother."

Shannon cringed. Her mother's tone implied that she wasn't in a good mood. No doubt about it, she still hadn't forgiven Shannon for taking this job.

Shannon's gaze flew to the man who'd stepped into her living room. Guilt riddled her for his mere presence in her home. Her mother would have a coronary if she knew Shannon had allowed a man like him into her house.

"Shannon?"

Shannon mentally shook herself, wondering what her mother would say if she could have witnessed Shannon's mesmerized reaction to a total stranger who also likely had a criminal record. "Yes, yes, I'm here."

"Have I caught you at a bad time?" her mother asked. What she meant was, "Are you so busy dancing with the devil down in that den of iniquity, that you don't have time to talk to your mother?"

Looking at the man who wandered her living room, Shannon decided the honest answer would be, "Well, we haven't danced together yet, but don't rule it out." What she said was, "I . . . did just get home from work."

"I see. How's your new job going?"

Shannon might have been able to answer that question intelligently if Rick Hardison hadn't at that very moment reached out and touched a daisy from the bouquet of flowers

Mark had sent her. That brought her attention to his hands. He had long, almost elegant fingers and strong-looking wrists. Those powerful hands probably had the strength to strangle her easily, if he wanted to. Or make her quiver with pleasure, if he wanted to. She had an insane desire to ask him if he wanted to.

"Shannon?"

"Oh . . . yes?"

"What's wrong with you?"

*I'm lusting after a potential guest star of AMERICA'S MOST WANTED is what's wrong with me.* "Nothing, Mother. I just . . . just walked in the door."

Rick Hardison's eyes lifted to hers . . . very slowly, as he made a few less than subtle pit stops on the trip up.

Her body flushed hotly in the places where his gaze had rested, and when she looked into his eyes, she held her breath. She'd never read such blatant, masculine desire in her life. He didn't even try to mask it.

"Mark came to supper last night," her mother said.

Shannon flinched. She really did feel badly about hurting Mark.

" . . . I cannot believe you never told us he proposed."

*Oh, no.* "He . . . told you?"

"Of course he told us! He thought we knew! Imagine our embarrassment when we had no idea what he was talking about!"

"I can't talk about this now, Mother."

There was a long, accusing silence. Into that silence came the sound of Rick Hardison clearing his throat. The noise sounded sexy as hell, vibrating along her nerve endings. Getting turned on by a dark stranger while conversing with her mother felt just a little too depraved. "I have to go. I love you. Talk to you soon," she said, then hung up the phone, her hands shaking.

The man walked over to her, his gait a sexy swagger. He stopped a few feet in front of her. Too close. And way too far away.

His dark eyes gleamed like polished black jewels, and the message in them was very, very clear. Even a relatively inexperienced woman like Shannon would have a tough time mistaking it.

He wanted to use her as a sex toy. There was no emotion behind the desire. He hadn't instantly fallen in love with her. He might not even like her if he got to know her. But there was only one way he wanted to get to know her, and it had nothing to do with personalities and everything to do with libidos.

"I'm all yours," Shannon whispered.

If her capitulation surprised him, he didn't show it. His slight smile was filled with self-confidence, which led her to the conclusion that Rick Hardison was used to getting what he wanted just by shooting a woman one smoldering look. He took easy conquests for granted.

The thought of being lumped into the category of Rick Hardison's easy conquests brought Shannon to her senses. She pressed her fingers to her lips and stumbled back a step. "Oh, my God, I didn't mean that! I don't know what came over me. I . . . I . . . you better go. Now. This minute. I . . . didn't mean it."

"Too bad."

Those two rumbled words plummeted like twin lead weights through her body, landing somewhere in her lower belly. Shannon dropped her hand. "I'm sorry. See, what happened is," she rushed on, desperate to explain, "King trapped me this morning and I was really scared and I started thinking about all the things I wanted to do that I might never do if King killed me. I've recently sort of had this fantasy about having a fling with a bad boy just once before I settle down, and then you showed up and you definitely look like the bad boy type, so I . . . got confused for a moment, and I . . . I . . . oh God!"

She covered her flaming face with her hands, willing herself to disappear in a puff of smoke. She couldn't believe she was capable of acting like such a complete idiot.

Suddenly she felt his fingers on her wrist, warm, electrifying. "Shannon," he said softly. "Don't apologize. I like fitting the image of your fantasy."

"Just get your dog and go."

Gently but firmly, he pulled one hand from her face. She kept her eyes squeezed tightly shut, on the theory that if she couldn't see him, he couldn't see her. Irrational, yes. But nothing about this situation smacked of rational.

"No," he said.

She didn't know if the dizzying pace of her blood flow stemmed from fear or excitement. She popped one eye open to look at him.

If it wasn't fear, it should have been. His presence overwhelmed her. He was dangerously huge, dangerously dark, and dangerously sexy.

"Please," she said, although she didn't exactly know what she was asking for.

"My pleasure," he murmured, then pulled her into his arms.

Shannon's hands got trapped between his ribs and her chest. She stared up at him, wondering if she should scream. And if she did scream, what would he do to shut her up? And if she didn't scream, what did that say about her moral fiber?

His heart beat slowly, steadily under her fingertips. In contrast, hers threatened to jackhammer its way out of her chest cavity. She wondered if he could feel or hear its rapid cadence.

This was pure insanity. She'd known this man for a total of ten minutes, tops, and she was already in his arms and seriously close to allowing him to seduce her.

Her brave words this morning had no basis in reality. No matter how dark her fantasies, she just didn't have it in her to have casual sex with a man. Not even this man. Her one and only partner had been Mark, and she'd dated him for nearly two years before she'd allowed their relationship to progress to that level of intimacy.

"Show me," he said, his voice low and growly.

"What?"

"Show me where my dog trapped you."

His eyes mesmerized her. They were so dark, opaque, but there was an ages-old wisdom in them, too. "Out back" she said, her voice faint.

His arms dropped from around her. Shannon almost shivered from the sudden lack of his warmth. She tried to slap a cool, distant smile on her face, as if she hadn't just been in his arms moments ago, contemplating a quick romp with him on the living room floor.

He smiled, which had such a startling effect on his features, Shannon nearly gasped. His grin didn't soften the harsh contours of his face, but instead sharpened them even further. He looked at once more alarming and more handsome. "Take me."

She considered that an excellent suggestion. But she was only vaguely aware of why. She was too busy deciding how tall he stood—a few inches above six feet was her guess. Which made him close to a foot taller than she.

"Shannon?"

"What?"

"Take me there."

Giving herself a mental slap, she asked, "Where?"

"Show me where he trapped you."

"Why?"

"Because he does that for only one reason, and I want to check it out."

"What one reason is that?"

"You sure you want to know?"

"Yes."

He shrugged. "He only acts that way when he's trying to protect someone from danger."

THE WAY Shannon Walsh's face drained of all color told Rick she'd changed her mind about wanting to know. And Rick hadn't even elaborated. If Bert acted strongly enough to frighten Shannon that much, then he'd been extremely concerned about her welfare.

It also explained why he'd jumped his own fence.

Rick searched for reassuring words, but he didn't have much practice giving beautiful women reassurances. Especially women he wanted to get down and dirty with in the worst way.

22

"Show me, Shannon," he murmured again, trying to ignore the painful tightening in his groin. He'd taken one look at prudish little Shannon Walsh and wanted to walk in, pick her up and cart her to the nearest expanse large enough to hold two writhing bodies.

He'd been instantly attracted to women before, but not to this magnitude. And he was so used to women who hid their honest desires behind cunning and manipulation that he hadn't been prepared for the naked plea that had screamed at him from the depths of Shannon's wide blue eyes.

But he also knew her type. She had commitment written all over that pretty little forehead of hers. And if there was one thing Rick now ran from, it was commitment. There was a basic equation he'd learned from his marriage. Commitment equaled living hell.

So, it was just as well she backed off. He was enough of a bastard to take her and walk away, but he wouldn't have enjoyed himself half so much if he worried about the aftermath, and hurting her. No, he had to stay away from commitment-minded Shannon Walsh.

But he didn't have to stay away from the Shannon Walsh who wanted to indulge in a fling. In fact, he was going to do everything in his power to bring that side of her out. That was the side he wanted to get naked with.

Damn, she was good-looking. Her eyes could make a man beg to swim in their clear blue depths. And her eyes weren't even her best feature. That honor, by far, went to her body. Even wearing a no-nonsense black skirt and white blouse, he could tell she was slight and slender, with a tiny waist and gently flaring hips.

Down at the station, Rick was known as a connoisseur of breasts. He could correctly guess any woman's bra size with just a glance. Shannon Walsh was a deliciously perfect thirty-four B.

She had a delicate frame, he knew, just from glimpsing her collar bone. And covering that frame was about the creamiest, silkiest looking skin he'd ever wanted to touch.

Her blonde hair was fairly short and curly. She probably

hated it for being impossibly unruly. Rick loved it for that very reason. Her hair gave her the look of a woman who'd just spent the better part of a wild night in bed.

He liked her lips a lot, too. Not too full, not too thin, they looked soft and rosy and exceedingly kissable. As did the small cleft in her chin. As did her pert nose. As did the golden, finely arched brows above those impossibly blue eyes.

Yes, indeed, Rick wanted Shannon Walsh. Just as soon as he got her to see the merit of having an affair with her neighbor. Her bad boy neighbor.

He nearly grinned. Well, she'd pegged him right off the bat. He was a bad boy, all right. His background hadn't given him much choice. No matter how much his grandfather had tried to "fix" him after he found him, it hadn't changed him. As his grandfather had finally conceded with a sigh, he could take the boy off the streets, but he couldn't take the street out of the boy.

He suddenly became aware that they'd been staring at each other again. He didn't think he'd ever experienced this instant rush of chemistry with a female before. He could take one look at a woman and decide whether he'd like to sleep with her, but he'd never taken one look and decided he *needed* to sleep with her.

"Show me where B—Hard On trapped you," he repeated, because the look on her face told him she'd forgotten the request.

She blinked, her eyes cleared and then narrowed. "Oh . . . right."

Rick bit his cheek to keep from grinning. He'd tell her Bert's real name. Eventually.

Turning, she led him through a pretty little living room into a small, cozy kitchen. Rick's eyes fastened on her swaying hips. Yeow!

She opened the back door. Rick put his hand on it and stepped back. "After you."

He followed her out. Unlike his place, she had a solid, knotty pine fence, and a neatly trimmed yard. She had pots of flowers everywhere and she had a small vegetable garden. Rick's fence was steel, his yard an unruly mess, and the only plant in it was an ancient sugar maple the last owners had left behind.

Bert yelped and turned in dizzying circles at the sight of him. Rick couldn't help but smile. The unconditional adoration his dog provided never failed to touch his heart in a way no human could. Bert didn't care if Rick came from the streets, didn't care if Rick often resembled the dregs of humanity he spent far too much time around.

Shannon unhooked what looked like a clothesline from Bert's collar, laughing as Bert worked hard to lave her face with his tongue. At the moment, Rick found himself unenviably jealous of his dog.

"You big marshmallow." She scratched Bert behind the ears, then straightened.

First a creampuff, then a marshmallow. Rick would have liked to take offense on Bert's behalf. Too bad it was the truth.

Shannon looked at Rick, an impish grin on her face that did something funny to his chest. "You did a real good job of training him," she said.

Bert romped to Rick, slurped his hand once, then the fickle mutt whirled and headed back to Shannon. Rick supposed he couldn't blame him. If he had a choice, he'd pick Shannon to lick every single time.

Briefs or boxers? The first words out of her mouth. Of course, she'd immediately looked mortified. What sort of woman was Shannon Walsh? he wondered. On the surface, he'd have pegged her as a woman who'd led a pristine life, and had finally figured out that pristine wasn't all it was cracked up to be. She was experimenting with her dark side.

Of course, he'd stopped trusting his judgment when it came to women and their motives. After all, hadn't he thought Mary Anne loved him for who he was?

Rick shook his head. He'd stopped trying to dissect the female psyche long ago. He'd never understand them. But, man-oh-man how he loved to touch them.

"Sit, Har—doggy," Shannon said, dragging Rick back to the present. Bert dutifully handed her his paw. Rick supposed he should be embarrassed by Bert's less than stellar performance in the tricks department, but the sound of Shannon's delighted laughter made the humiliation worthwhile.

She glanced from Bert to Rick, her smile socking him in the gut. "Did you train him this way on purpose?"

Rick was tempted to lie, but her open, guileless expression—whether a facade or not—compelled him toward honesty. "Not exactly."

She tilted her head. "How did he learn everything wrong?"

Rick descended the steps, feeling some kind of invisible force drawing him inexorably toward her. "He's a K-9 Corps reject."

She tilted her head the other way. At an angle for their lips to fit together perfectly if he bent to kiss her. Damn, he really wanted to kiss her.

"You mean, he's a police dog?" she asked.

"He was supposed to be. He flunked out."

She looked at Bert. "Roll over!"

Bert obediently dropped into his death pose.

Shannon laughed softly. "He's adorable."

"He's not really dumb," Rick defended. "His trainer knew he'd never make it as a K-9. So when I asked to have him, the trainer thought it would be real funny to teach him this way. I didn't want to confuse him, so I never tried to change him."

Her eyes shone bright blue. She looked at him in a way that one could interpret as admiration, if one wanted to be foolish enough to do so. "That's cute."

*Cute? Cute!* Rick had been called a lot of rotten things in his life. By far, "cute" ranked as the worst. He decided to disabuse her of this cute thing right up front.

He graced her with the grin that had convinced many a woman to part with her panties. Her smile evaporated. Her eyes went wide. She looked like she was torn between running like hell and flinging herself at him.

The uncertainty in her eyes made him back off. He didn't mind taking advantage of women who made it real clear what they wanted from him. Taking advantage of one who didn't know what she wanted smacked of emotional rape.

Dragging his gaze from her parted lips, he looked across her back yard to his. Because of her fence and the sloping hill, only the upper level of his house was visible. Well, no wonder she hadn't recognized Bert. And it was also no wonder that the two of them hadn't run into each other. He'd been immersed in putting an end to Lucky Louie's bookmaking ways the last couple of weeks, barely taking the time to come home.

Well, that had all changed this morning. Since he'd be working normal hours again for the next few weeks, he'd have plenty of time to convince Shannon Walsh that he was the answer to her prayers. He looked forward to it.

"Show me where he trapped you," he said.

"I came out to hang some . . . clothing on the clothesline," Shannon said, turning her back on him to point.

Holy sh—

She swung back to face him, and caught him in mid-stare. When he finally managed to raise his gaze, he found her cheeks ripening with color.

"But . . . King was standing here, snarling at me." She shuddered. "I don't know how he got in."

Rick started across the lawn. "Stay, B—Hard On."

Bert came bounding after him.

Rick grinned as he heard Shannon cluck her disgust behind him. He skirted the neatly tended garden, searching the ground. Nothing. He unlatched the brass hook, swinging the gate open. There was about a ten foot expanse of grass between Shannon's back fence and his. It was neatly mowed, and Rick assumed Shannon took care of it, because he knew he certainly didn't.

Bert bounded through the gate ahead of him and raced directly to a crabapple tree, standing just outside the far right edge of Shannon's fence.

Rick approached it, his eyes sweeping the ground. In the middle of summer, small crabapples already littered the grass. Hunkering down, he noticed some crushed fruit in different spots around the base of the tree. Someone, recently, had walked by or stood under the tree.

Not much of a clue, considering there were plenty of children in the neighborhood, and this gnarled old tree would make a great climber. Still, he didn't like that Bert seemed so concerned about Shannon. There had to have been some kind of danger out here somewhere.

He looked around some more, but found nothing else unusual. Returning to Shannon, he found her in her garden, busy picking tomatoes and peppers.

She glanced up when he latched the gate. "Well?"

Rick shrugged. She looked adorable with her hair blowing and bouncing in the breeze. He knew a swift, intense need to turn into a caveman, haul her sexy little butt over his shoulder and lug her into his lair. He focused on the tomatoes, trying to fight the desire crashing through him. "Someone's been back there recently, but it could have been kids."

She nipped at her lower lip. "I'm sure there's nothing to worry about."

Rick disagreed with that assessment, but he preferred to be the one to worry. "Right. Just remember to keep your doors and windows locked up tight."

He thought about offering Bert's services for a few days, but he wasn't certain she wouldn't get a false sense of security. Bert had flunked out of the police academy because of his irritating ability to love everyone, including bad guys. Although Bert seemed unusually protective of Shannon, Rick didn't know if he wouldn't be equally fond of a prowler.

Shannon started toward the house. "Well, it was kind of you to check out there for me . . ."

*Now go away.* She didn't say it, but the words hung in the air anyway. As he and Bert followed her into the house, Rick considered his next move. And for the first time in his life, he was at a loss.

The summer sun had set, and ribbons of red and orange streaked across the sky. Somewhere in the neighborhood, folks barbecued some mouth-watering meat. Rick's stomach rumbled.

In the kitchen Shannon dumped her bounty, and briskly headed to the living room and the front door. She put her hand on the knob and turned, a cheerful, fake-as-paste-jewels smile on her face. "Well, thanks again!"

Rick stopped in front of her. "I'm the one who should thank you for taking care of my dog."

"You're welcome."

She looked everywhere but into his eyes, making it impossible for Rick to re-establish the bond they'd felt earlier. For some reason, that irritated him. "I'd like to repay you."

Her gaze flew up and collided with his. "Oh, that's not at all necessary."

"Yeah, I think it is," he said, his eyes wandering down to her breasts, then back up.

"No, really," she said, her voice going breathy.

"I insist."

He cupped her neck and brushed his thumb along her jaw. While she stared up at him with eyes as big as the Atlantic and Pacific, he lowered his lips to hers. He meant to take just a small sip, a small taste. And he tried. He really did. He searched for control and came up empty.

His free hand lifted to trap her head, and he slanted their lips, pressed hers apart and stabbed his tongue into her mouth. She went stiff.

Rick lifted his head. "Kiss me back," he growled.

"You should go," she whispered.

"I'm not leaving until you kiss me back."

She opened her mouth to protest. Rick didn't give her the chance. He pressed his lips to hers again. After an uncertain moment, she relaxed and gave him her full participation. And when little Shannon Walsh decided to participate, she didn't do it halfway.

Her hands slid up his ribs to his chest, then around his neck. Her lips brushed his passionately, her tongue explored his mouth. Rick grasped her waist and pulled her against him, and he groaned when her soft breasts pressed against his ribs.

He wanted to devour her, taste every inch of her. He wanted her naked and open beneath him, hot and wet and ready. He wanted her shapely thighs gripping his hips as their bodies ground together in a rhythm as old as time. He wanted her breasts in his mouth, her scent in his nostrils, her moans of ecstasy in his ears.

He kissed her throat and neck, savoring her female skin. His hands explored the contours of her body, learning her shape. He liked what he learned. He liked it a lot.

"Look at me," he demanded, his voice hoarse.

Her eyes fluttered open, and the passion in them made his knees go weak and other parts go rock-hard.

"It's inevitable, you know."

"Wh . . . what?"

"Us." His hand skimmed up her waist to the side of her breast. He brushed his thumb across her already peaked nipple. "This."

She inhaled sharply and visibly jumped. Rick managed to stand still, even though everything inside him jumped as well. God, he wanted this woman. Now.

Her eyes cleared to a sky blue, and he knew the moment she came to the conclusion that kissing him had been a horrible mistake. She pushed at his chest, and he let her go. Very, very reluctantly, he let her go.

She fussed with her blouse. "Well, Mr. Hardison . . . well, goodbye."

He tipped up her chin. "You want it as much as I do."

"No, I—"

"Didn't your mother teach you not to lie?"

She jerked her chin from his grasp. "What my mother taught me was to stay far, far away from men like you."

He shot her an indolent grin. "Sage advice."

"My thoughts exactly."

"So tell me, Ms. Walsh," he said, brushing back a blonde curl from her cheek, "if it's such good advice, and you're such a smart lady, how come you want me so bad?" He held up a hand to forestall her retort. "You've got my number. When you decide you're ready for that fling, give me a call." He looked down at Bert. "Stay!"

Then they walked out of the house and down the sidewalk,

Rick never looking back. Whistling, he shoved his hands in his coat pockets so she wouldn't see them clenched in frustrated fists.

"WHAT'S WRONG with you today?" Diane asked Shannon the next afternoon at lunch.

Shannon rearranged the lettuce and tomatoes in her taco salad. She shrugged. "Problem with a neighbor. At least, I think we're neighbors."

"What kind of problem?" Diane asked after swallowing a bite of chicken burrito and washing it down with iced tea.

Shannon looked at her friend. When one met Diane Mackenzie, one word came to mind: robust. She did everything with gusto; eat, drink, swear and dress. She had big hair, loud clothes and an unquenchable thirst for men. And men seemed to return the favor in droves. In other words, she was absolutely nothing like Shannon.

But Shannon liked and trusted Diane. Diane was the only person in the world she'd confessed her secret fantasy to. Well, except for Rick Hardison. And just like Rick Hardison, Diane was determined to get Shannon to fulfill it.

"Remember I told you about the dog?"

"Uh-huh," Diane said, sounding disinterested.

"Well, the guy who owns him came to get him last night."

Diane perked up. "And?"

"And he wants to . . . to . . ."

"Play Scrabble?"

"No."

"Go to dinner?"

"No. He doesn't even want to bother with that intro."

"He wants to go straight into doing the nasty?"

"Yes."

"Oh, baby, this is cool!"

"No, it's not."

"Why not? Is he ugly?"

"He's gorgeous."

"Is he short?"

"Tall."

"Bald?"

"Dark, thick hair down to his shoulders."

"Does he drool?"

"Not that I've noticed."

"Dumb as a brick?"

"Too smart for my own good."

Diane growled her exasperation. "Then what's the problem? Run, don't walk, to the bedroom."

"He's all wrong for me."

Diane's jaw nearly hit the table. "Tall, dark and handsome is all wrong for you?"

"He's . . . " Shannon waved. " . . . probably got a rap sheet a mile long."

"What, did he show up in prison fatigues?"

"The next best thing. If I saw him on the street, I'd bet he was a gang leader or something."

"Oooh, yummy! I love those dark and dangerous types. Go for it."

"He wears an earring."

"And this is a problem because . . . ?"

Shannon's nose tilted skyward. "I don't date men who wear earrings."

"Did he ask you out?"

"No."

"Then he's not asking you to date him, dummy. Go ahead and stick to your Dudley Do-Right plans for the future. Just bed the man." With that sound advice, Diane re-applied herself to her burrito.

Shannon stabbed at her salad irritably. Problem was, she was thinking about it. In fact, she'd thought of nothing else since Rick Hardison had ambled down her sidewalk last night, so damned cocky and sure of himself, she'd wanted to throw her shoe at the back if his pony-tailed head.

Then she'd spent the next couple of hours desperately trying to forget his phone number. When that hadn't happened, she'd caved into the inevitable and started rationally considering her options.

She'd mentally listed the pros and cons of having an affair with him. The only pro had been her certainty that he was an animal in bed. And, God help her, she wanted to experience—just once in her boring life—sex at the hands of an animal.

The "con" side of the list could take pages. A loveless affair went against everything her strict Presbyterian upbringing had taught her. Especially a loveless affair with a man who was so obviously wrong for her. The affair wouldn't, couldn't, lead to anything permanent.

But then, wasn't that what she wanted?

On the other hand, what did she know about the man? That he loved animals, especially his dog. He'd been frantic to get Hard On back. The sum total of her knowledge of Rick Hardison. She didn't know if he had any diseases she should worry about, didn't know if he had a girlfriend, or, God forbid, a wife. He hadn't worn a ring, but that didn't mean a thing. Rick Hardison didn't strike her as a man who'd wear a symbol of commitment. And he'd been awfully determined to keep her from bringing his dog to his home.

A thought hit her. "What if he uses that dog to meet single women?"

Diane waved her fork. "Tall, dark and handsome types don't need to use a dog to get women."

"True. Still, Har—King showed up again this morning."

"King?"

"The dog."

"Is he still at your house, or did you send him home?"

"I don't know where 'home' is. I don't think he wanted me to know."

"It's fate. Call him and when he shows up tear off his clothes."

Unfortunately, that sounded like a wonderful idea. "No, I'm not going to get involved with a criminal, no matter how good-looking Rick Hardison is."

Diane's fork clattered as it missed her Spanish rice and hit the plate. "What did you say?"

"I said—"

"What's the name of your mystery man?"

Shannon noted Diane's heightened color with interest. "Rick Hardison."

"Oh, my God!"

"You know him?"

Diane held her hand flat, several inches above her head. "Six feet-three or so inches of testosterone?"

"Yes."

"Dark eyes that scream, 'I can make your every dream come true?'"

"Yes."

"Lips that look like they've been sculpted with kissing in mind?"

"Yes."

"Shoulders out to here?"

"Yes."

Diane threw back her head and laughed.

"What?"

Eyes swimming with moisture, Diane finally got her laughter under control. "Go to bed with him."

"Why?"

"Honey, you've just been handed a godsend, and you don't even know it."

"Why?"

"Because every female in the greater DC area, young and old, married or not, would give their eye teeth to get within spitting distance of that man's bed."

"What are you talking about?"

"Rick Hardison ain't no criminal."

"He's not?"

"He's not. Although, men that sexy probably ought to be outlawed."

"He sure looks like a criminal to me."

"Well, he's not. Fact is, he's a cop."

# Chapter Three

"YOU'RE A COP!" Shannon spat at Rick accusingly, the moment she opened the door to him.

His eyebrows shot up. "Been checking up on me, little Shannon?"

She crossed her arms and gave him a disgusted once over. Still, she didn't quite manage to hide her surprise.

She wasn't the only surprised person in this crowd. Rick had never dressed to impress in his life. Tonight, before coming to pick up Bert, he'd not only showered and shaved, he'd also pulled out what he considered his dress jeans—the only pair he owned that didn't have holes in them. He'd also worn a button down shirt instead of his standard T-shirt, and he'd thrown his Nautica jacket overtop that.

The moment he'd come home and gotten Shannon's message, he'd even felt a strong urge to go out and get a haircut.

Which ticked him off.

Making himself over for a woman went against everything he believed. It was the reason his marriage had lasted less than a year. Mary Anne had wanted to change everything about him, from the way he dressed to the way he talked to the way he made love.

Rick suppressed a shudder. Trying to please her had driven him halfway insane. Never again. Never, never again.

"What monumental ego!" Shannon breathed. "No, I was not checking up on you. As a matter of fact, I was complaining about you to my boss."

Grinning, he said, "Mack? You complained about me to Mack?"

She nodded grudgingly.

"And just what did Mack say about me?"

Shannon blushed. Which gave him a pretty good idea what Mack had said about him. He'd known Diane Mackenzie for years, ever since he'd been a rookie beat cop. Although they'd often joked about having an affair, Rick had never pursued the idea seriously. He liked Mack too much to risk the friendship.

While still blushing, Shannon managed to glare at him. "She said you're a conceited jerk who thinks he can take one look at a woman and she'll breathlessly fall into your arms."

"Like you did?"

Her jaw came unhinged. "Why you . . . you . . ."

Rick crossed his arms, waiting for her to come up with an apt description. This wasn't going the way he'd planned. He hadn't meant to make her mad, but she looked so pretty when vibrating with indignation, he hadn't been able to stop himself.

" . . . cop!" she finally said. Somehow she made it sound like an epithet.

He wondered if she had a thing against cops.

"You didn't mention you were a cop yesterday," she added.

"You didn't ask."

"You're not a bad boy at all. You're one of the good guys."

How she managed to make that sound like a bad thing, he didn't know. "Oh, I wouldn't be quick to assume too much, Shannon, honey. Even guys with badges have their dark sides. Want a demonstration?"

Her accusatory frown turned to alarm right quick. She backed up. "No!"

Rick followed her into the house. "Sure about that?"

"Yes."

"Let me see if I understand this," he said, still stalking her. "When you thought I was a thug, you were attracted to me. Now that you know I'm a cop, you've lost interest."

"I was never attracted to you."

"Right."

"Well, maybe a little, but I'm over it now."

"Right."

"Well, maybe not, but it's under control."

"Right."

She backed up to a chair and dropped into it. "It is."

Rick leaned over her, bracing his hands on the arms of the chair. "Give me five minutes with that luscious little body of yours, baby, and you won't be able to spell the word control."

Her breasts—underneath another prissy little white blouse—rose and fell with her increasingly rapid breaths. "You're very conceited, you know."

"No, I'm very determined. When I see something I want, I go after it." He swept his gaze down her body. Today she wore a dusky pink skirt, short enough to reveal her knees. He'd never realized he was a knee man, but he really liked hers. "And right now, I see something I want very, very much."

"Har . . . d, er, On's out back," she said weakly.

"No, hard on's right here."

Shannon blew a disgusted breath. "Why does he keep coming here?"

"He's trying to protect you."

"If he wants to protect me, he should be in here standing between you and me."

Rick chuckled. "Are you afraid of me, Shannon?"

"Oh, yes."

He straightened. Her wide eyes and shallow breaths told him she meant it. He didn't like her being afraid of him. "You have nothing to worry about. I've never forced myself on a woman, and I'm not going to start with you."

She looked visibly relieved. Which also ticked him off. So he leaned toward her again, and ran his index finger lightly down the small cleft in her chin. God, she had fantastic skin—creamy looking and baby soft. "Fair warning. That doesn't mean I'm not going to do whatever it takes to get you to go to bed with me."

Her relief vanished. "Why?"

"Honey, you were there right along with me last night. The fireworks flying could have lit up DC. And they weren't flying one way."

"But, you don't know anything about me."

"I know a lot of things about you. I know that your big blue eyes are about the prettiest I've ever seen. I know that you've got a body that could turn on a cadaver. I know your lips are soft and sweet and your skin smells like heaven. I know that I'm going to die a very unhappy man if I buy the farm without ever experiencing what it feels like to be inside you."

She swallowed. Hard. Twice. "That's . . . all superficial stuff. I mean, you don't know anything about my personality."

"It's not your personality I want to have sex with."

She gaped up at him. "That's disgusting."

His finger traced her jaw. "But honest." He straightened again. "How about you being a little honest, here, Shannon? If you could have sex with me without any dire consequences, wouldn't you want to?"

She hesitated. "Yes."

"Because of my brain?"

"Because you're . . . exciting."

"Why?"

"I . . . don't know. Maybe it has something to do with forbidden candy or something"

"Works for me. Let's do it."

"No," she said, shaking her head. "I can't have . . . relations with a stranger."

Relations? Where had this woman grown up? In a convent, was Rick's first guess. "I'm an open book. What do you want to know?"

"Well, the first thing that comes to mind is your health record. Have any diseases?"

"Chicken Pox when I was seven."

"You know what I mean."

"Yes, I do. And, no, I don't."

"Am I supposed to just take your word for that?"

Rick shrugged. "You're the scientist. Draw some of my blood and test it." He grinned. "How about you?"

Her nose shot skyward. "Of course not."

"Good. Let's have sex."

Her mouth dropped open. Then she shook her head and laughed. "You're crazy."

"Yeah, but I bet crazy is exactly what you want, isn't it?"

She stared at him, mute.

Smiling, he said, "You've never had it crazy, have you?"

She pressed her lips together. Rick had to keep from laughing. Because as out of line as he'd gotten, as rude as he'd acted, he could see the glimmer of anticipation in her eyes. And it drove him wild. "Oh, yeah, we'll be good together, Shannon. Real good."

It took every ounce of willpower he possessed to walk away from her. "I'll get Hard On, and we'll go out the back way. Have a nice night, angel."

He turned toward the kitchen, but not before he saw disappointment cloud her features. He had to stop himself from punching the air in victory.


TEN HOURS LATER, Rick wasn't feeling so victorious. For the first time in weeks he'd looked forward to a full eight hours of sleep. Unfortunately, thoughts of Shannon Walsh and how good they could be together had kept him tossing deep into the night. He couldn't ever remember losing sleep over a woman before.

He supposed he'd been celibate too long. Otherwise, how could he explain this strange and strong attraction to the lady? Sure, she was great-looking, but the prissy types had never been his style.

Yet he'd taken one look at prim and proper little Shannon, and bang! An instant chemical explosion had erupted inside him. He wondered if it had something to do with his wanting what he couldn't have.

He considered wanting things he couldn't have his most basic personality flaw. That yearning had been responsible for some of the biggest mistakes in his life. Like his marriage. Like a few un-wise juvenile pranks, several of which had landed him in the hands of the Chicago police.

Rick punched his pillow and rolled over. The sheet twisted around his hips, but he didn't care. He closed his eyes and willed himself to sleep.

Bert's low, menacing growl brought him upright. He looked to his left. Bert stood at his bedroom window. He'd nudged aside the blind and was riveted by something in the back yard.

Rick kicked off the sheet and walked naked to the window. He raised the blind and grabbed the binoculars he'd left on the dresser the night before, intending to keep an eye on Shannon Walsh.

He brought them to his eyes and sought out the crabapple tree. From his second story vantage point he had an unobstructed view of both yards, but in the pre-dawn darkness he had trouble seeing anything.

"What is it, Bert?"

Bert whined.

Rick's gaze moved to Shannon's back yard. That's when he noticed the light on in a room at the back of the house. Shannon was awake too, apparently. Again he swept the yard and the grassy lane between their fences. Nothing.

He looked back at the lit window. And nearly dropped his binoculars. Shannon stood just inside it, her profile to him. Must be the bathroom, he decided, when he realized she was brushing her teeth.

She wore a bright red camisole, and her hair was all mussed. Seeing her like that conjured images of her sleep-flushed body, and he tore his gaze from the window, gritting his teeth as desire flooded him.

Didn't the fool woman know to close her blinds? Any pervert could be gaping at her right now.

He checked out the yards again. Again he saw nothing. Dawn was finally leaching the darkness from the sky, turning it from purple to violet.

Before he could stop himself, he looked back at Shannon's bathroom. In time to catch her lifting off her camisole.

"My God!" he whispered.

She disappeared a moment later, presumably into the shower. But for that instant, he'd seen Shannon Walsh in all her naked glory. From her waist up, at any rate. And, Lord, he'd enjoyed the view.

Swearing under his breath, he dragged his gaze from the window. Self-disgust welled up in him. God, he'd stooped low before, but not low enough to act like a perverted voyeur.

Bert's low growl jerked him out of his bout of self-flagellation. He followed the direction of Bert's gaze. Sure enough, something moved in the crabapple tree. Something too large to be a squirrel or a bird. Something dressed in dark colors. Something that could also see into Shannon's bathroom.

Fury filled him. And a healthy fear for Shannon's welfare as well. "Let's get him, Bert," he said, whirling and snatching up his gun. Checking the clip, he started for the door. Fortunately he remembered his nakedness just in time. He threw on a pair of sweat pants then ran down the stairs.

At his back door he stopped. "Quiet, Bert."

He eased the door open. Bert bounded through, barking at the top of his lungs. Rolling his eyes, Rick ran after him.

Bert didn't even hesitate as he approached the fence. He sailed right over it like a horse. Prudently, Rick decided to use the gate.

Bert circled the crabapple tree wildly. Rick looked up at the lowest branch. Sitting in it, looking trapped and frightened, was a teenage boy.

"Attack!" Rick ordered.

The boy clutched at the tree.

Bert rolled to his back and stuck his four paws in the air.

"Relax," Rick said to the kid, keeping his gun hidden behind his back. "He's not going to hurt you."

The boy didn't look convinced.

"Who the hell are you, and what are you doing up in that tree?"

The boy lifted his chin belligerently, reminding Rick of

himself as a kid. "None o' yer damn business."

"I'm a cop, sonny boy. I'm making it my business."

If anything, the boy grew more defiant. He spat, a little too close to Rick's bare foot. "I hate cops."

"And I can't stand snotty little kids, so we're even. And lest we forget, I'm the one with the badge."

The boy shrugged. Oh, yes, he reminded Rick of himself at that age. Rick recognized the angry gleam in the boy's eyes. He softened his tone. "What's your name?"

The kid just scowled.

"Listen, bozo, you can either tell me your name now, or I can haul your scrawny ass down to the station and we can find out who you are there. I'll ask you one last time. What's your name?"

"Tony," the kid answered in a grudging tone.

"Tony what?"

"Mandello," Tony mumbled.

"Where do you live?"

Tony waved vaguely to his right.

"The address, Tony."

Tony spat out his address. He lived about a block west of Rick. Rick nodded. "Now tell me why you're spying on the lady."

"Go to hell."

Rick casually slipped his hair behind his ear, then reached out his hand and propped it against the tree trunk. "I didn't hear you, Tony. What'd you say?"

The boy's Adam's apple wobbled a little, but he kept the fierce, belligerent scowl firmly in place. "I been comin' here longer than she has," Tony said, jerking a thumb toward Shannon's house. I been comin' here for two years. It's not my fault the broad started strippin' in front of her window."

Rick nodded. "All right. I'm going to take your word for it this time. I mean, after all, it's pretty perverted to intentionally spy on a woman in her own home, huh?"

Tony didn't answer him.

"In fact, it's downright disgusting. They lock guys like that up all the time, and you wouldn't believe what other prisoners do to those pathetic creeps."

The boy squirmed.

"Go home. I'm going to be keeping an eye out here, Tony. Count on it. So don't ever let me catch you in that tree spying on the lady again. If you want to see naked women, find yourself a Playboy." Rick backed up a couple of steps, giving the kid room to escape. "Stay, Bert."

Bert jumped up and moved to Rick's side. "Lie down."

Bert sat.

"That dog is stupid."

"Maybe. But he knows how to tear snotty little kids to shreds."

Tony's bravado slipped a couple of notches.

"Go on, get out of here. He won't come after you."

The kid hesitated, then leapt from the tree and hit the ground running.

Rick watched him go. Then shaking his head, he turned to look at the back of Shannon's fence. "I think we need to go teach Miz Walsh a lesson. Stay."

He stalked to Shannon's gate, Bert trotting happily beside him. Before he could open it, Bert sailed over top. Rick blew his lips in disgust and unlatched the gate. As he stomped across Shannon's back yard, he let his temper flare. The fool woman! What did she think, that the people living behind her were all blind? What the hell was she doing, stripping in front of an open window?

He rapped on her back door with the heel of his hand. Then waited. And waited. He rapped again.

Shannon pulled the curtain from the door's window aside a mere inch and peeked out. Those big blue eyes got bigger and bluer. The curtain fell back into place and the door swung open.

"Rick? What are—" Her eyes swept his naked torso. "Oh, my God!" She wrapped her short red silky-looking robe tighter around her body. For as conservatively as she dressed during the day, she had at least a little wild streak in her at night. He liked that.

Her hair was still wet from a shower, but already curling around her face. She smelled fresh and clean, and her skin glowed from recent scrubbing. Rick's body responded like dry kindling to a flame at the sight and scent of her.

That's when he remembered he had his gun. No wonder she looked a little frightened.

"May I come in?" he asked, his mouth twisting in an ironic grin.

"Absolutely not!"

"We need to talk."

"Well that's just too bad. If you think I'd allow a half-naked, armed man into my house, you're crazy!"

He could smell coffee brewing. "You've got a peeping Tom, Shannon."

"What?"

"Please let me in so we can talk about it. I'm harmless, I swear." To prove it, he expelled the clip from his gun and held it up. "Disarmed."

She snorted and held out her hand. "Give it to me."

Rick dutifully handed her the clip. If any of his colleagues knew he'd done it, he'd get razzed to all hell.

Shannon stepped back. Which gave Rick an unobstructed view of her bare legs all the way up to shapely thighs. Without thinking, he whistled his appreciation.

Shannon immediately crossed her arms. "You are so crude."

Rick grinned. "Just enjoying the view." He looked down at Bert. "Come!" Bert immediately hunkered down and put his head between his paws. Satisfied, Rick stepped into the kitchen.

Shannon clucked her tongue. "Do women really fall for your lines?"

"I don't do lines, sweetheart. Takes too much effort."

"What are you doing, skulking around my backyard half-naked?"

She eyed his bare chest, attempting disdain . . . and failing. Her expressive face was as readable as a neon sign. The admiration that glowed in her eyes made him want to drag her to the floor and bury himself in her until nothing existed but their bodies, their senses, their heat.

"Like what you see?" he asked, after a long stretch in which she stared at him.

Shannon shook her head, trying to clear it. That didn't help. Not when his big wall of beautiful chest filled her doorway. For the first time in her life, Shannon had an overwhelming urge to kiss a man's nipples.

Her own nipples responded to the thought, beading and tingling. To hide their reaction, she raised her crossed arms higher.

She couldn't believe she'd allowed him into her home. Half-dressed, with his hair loose, he looked like a savage beast. A sexy, savage beast.

His sweat pants rode low on his hips. She tried very hard not to look down there, but it wasn't easy. In fact, finding a part of him to focus on was exceedingly difficult altogether. Every inch of him looked yummy and wicked from the tip of his head to the bare toes of his feet.

"It wouldn't take but a moment to undress me for real, you know."

Shannon's gaze jumped to his and she felt her cheeks go hot. "I . . . wasn't undressing you."

He shot her a lazy grin. "Honey, I almost felt my sweat pants drop."

Her chin jerked up. "Is there anyone in this world who thinks as highly of you as you do?"

"You?"

"In your dreams, buster. The weight of your ego could sink ships."

Rick shrugged one shoulder. "Ego or not, I know when a woman wants me."

Because denying it would be a lie, she changed the subject.

"I believe you mentioned something about a peeping Tom?"

"Right." He took the clip from her hand and laid it, along with the gun, on the counter. Then he grabbed her wrist and started dragging her toward the living room. "Come with me."

"Where are we going?"

"To your bathroom."

Shannon tried to dig in her heels. "Why?"

"Stop fighting me. I'm not going to ravish you, Shannon. I just want to show you something."

He drew her inexorably down the hallway, opening each door on the left side. When he came to the bathroom, he turned on the light and hauled her inside.

He took her shoulders and turned her toward the window. "What do you see out there?"

Shannon looked out, then tipped her head back. "Nothing. It's dark outside."

"Right." He flicked off the light. "Now what do you see?"

She looked out again. "My back yard."

"Do you see the crabapple tree?"

"Yes."

"Well, a few minutes ago, a hormonally charged adolescent young man was sitting in that crabapple tree looking in on you."

Shannon gasped. "Oh, my God!" She tipped her head back again. "Someone was *watching me?*"

"What did you expect when you're flashing that pretty little body in front of a window?" Rick said, his tone angry. He reached over her shoulder and pulled down the blind. His masculine scent hit her with the force of a sledgehammer. He smelled deliciously male, dangerous and seductive.

"There's a reason people put these things on their windows, Shannon. It's called privacy."

"Who would want to watch me?" she asked.

Rick snorted. He grabbed her shoulders and turned her to face him. "You cannot possibly be that naive," he said, his onyx eyes glittering. "About every male who still has a pulse, that's who."

Shannon flushed. It had never occurred to her that anyone could see into her window. She kept the blind open because she liked the cool dawn air to help wake her in the mornings. "I . . . I . . . I'll be more careful."

"You do that." His fingers skimmed down the length of her arms. "I had a little chat with your peeping Tom, but I don't know if I scared him enough for him to stay away. So don't give him any reason to be tempted."

"I . . . won't."

"Keep your blinds closed, Shannon."

"I will."

"Unless . . . " He grinned.

"Unless . . . what?" she asked suspiciously.

He again turned her toward the window and raised the blind. "See the blue two story down there?"

"Yes."

"See the middle window on the second floor?"

"Yes."

"That's my bedroom."

"Oh, my God!"

Her shoulders went stiff under his fingers. He resisted the urge to massage her muscles. He forced himself not to kiss the nape of her neck. He fought to keep his hands from moving to her breasts. "Howdy, neighbor," he said, his voice as tight as the knot in his groin.

She whirled around to gape up at him. "You were the one watching me."

He managed to look offended rather than guilty as charged. "I was watching out for you. I was trying to find out why B—my dog races over here every morning."

"But . . . but, you looked."

"Guilty."

"Oh, my God."

"If it's any consolation, I liked what I saw."

Jeez, her face was so easy to read. He didn't think he'd ever met a woman whose emotions were so clearly displayed in her eyes. Realizing he really liked that about her, he smiled. "If it'll make you feel better, go ahead and slap me."

She held her right wrist with her left hand, as if to stop it from swinging. "You deserve to be slapped."

"For what I'm thinking right now, you're probably right. But believe me, I had no idea you'd be stripping nude right in front of a window. It was an accident that I saw you."

The anger and embarrassment evaporated from her eyes. Curiosity bloomed instead. "What are you thinking right now?"

"You sure you want to hear it?"

She took about one-point-five seconds to decide. "Yes."

"I'm thinking, Lord, I've never wanted a woman like I want you."

"Oh." Her gaze dropped to his chest, then skittered away. "Would you like some coffee?"

He rubbed his stubbled jaw. "Let's see. I'm standing in a bathroom with a nearly naked woman who makes me crazy with lust. So my choices here are to either try and relieve her of the skimpy little robe she's wearing, or I can be a gentleman and kindly accept the offer of coffee." He tipped up her chin. "Which would you prefer? The scruffy cop or the gentleman?"

It actually took her a few moments to make up her mind. "The gentleman."

Sighing, he dropped his hand. "Fine. But, Shannon?"

"Yes?"

"Accept the fact that we're going to have sex with each other. It'll be easier on your nerves."

Her eyes flamed. "Has anyone ever said 'no' to you?"

"Many, many times," Rick said, his jaw locking up as he thought of his ex-wife.

"Then why can't you accept a 'no' from me?"

"I am accepting it. Right now, at any rate. I just think you'll change your mind." He grinned. "And when you do, just give me the signal, and I'll get here as fast as I can."

"Signal?"

Rick turned her back to the window. "When you decide you

want me, just raise this blind and leave the light on. Just don't strip in front of it."

She gazed up at him for a long, thoughtful moment. He could almost hear the motor chugging in her head. "If I ever decided to give the signal—I'm not saying I will—but if I did, it would only be one time, right?"

Rick thought he'd take her a whole lot more than once, but he'd handle that hurdle when he came to it. "Right."

"That's all it would be. Just a . . . fling."

"A brief affair," he agreed.

"Because . . . because there'd be no future."

Rick considered that a bonus, but for some reason it irritated him that she'd voiced it. "Don't worry, doll. I'm not my dog. I have no desire to have a collar locked around my throat."

She nodded. "I'm glad we agree. Because, well, frankly, you're all wrong for me."

Why that bothered him, Rick couldn't say. But it did. "Is that right?"

She nodded again, and started to say more, but Rick was in no mood to hear her list his shortcomings. He hauled her against him, then took her mouth, ignoring the gasp in her throat.

He kissed her, surprised by the stunning need that curled, then fisted, in the pit of his stomach. Aware only that she didn't fight him, Rick mindlessly ravished her mouth. Kissing a woman had never had such a startling effect on him that he could remember. Arousal flashed through his body, throbbing painfully in his groin.

He had to stop. This was madness. He wasn't prepared to protect her, and he was excited enough he might take her too roughly. It wasn't supposed to have happened this way. He had to stop.

While he held her at the nape, trapped against his devouring lips, his other hand fumbled with the silk sash at her waist. When he got it untied, he pushed her robe aside and palmed her breast.

She made a soft clicking sound, but she didn't stop him. Damn, he wished she'd fight him, slap him, kick him. Instead she arched into his palm and clutched his arms.

Her acquiescence, her surrender, her participation, all fueled a raging passion that engulfed him. He had to have her. He had to stop.

He had to stop.

Rick tore his mouth from hers and looked down at her, praying she'd appear so frightened she'd douse his painful need for her.

No such luck. Her eyes were wide, but with wonder, not fear. Her lips were parted and swollen and moist. He might have found a way to ignore all of that and just walk away, if he didn't make the mistake of glancing down at her exposed breast. It was perfect, high and round and creamy with a small dusky pink nipple.

Rick hissed a curse, then grabbed a handful of her hair and pulled her head back. His lips traveled down her delicate, exposed throat to her collar, then her breast. She gasped as he took it deep into his mouth, sucking like a greedy, hungry child.

Or a greedy, hungry man.

Her hands clutched his head, her lips moaned his name. Her body started quivering under his fingers, his lips.

Through the fog of desire in his brain, his conscience began to emerge. *She hasn't said "yes" yet, buddy. She hasn't given the signal. You're forcing her, whether she's fighting you or not.*

With more reluctance than he'd feel shooting himself, Rick managed to release her breast. It glistened and puckered from his cherishing. Gritting his teeth, he covered her up and re-tied her belt.

"Rick?"

He made himself look at her. Her eyes were passion-fuzzy, dazed. Her lower lip trembled, and she caught it between her teeth. "Is . . . something wrong?" she asked, her voice breathy and husky all at once.

His stomach muscles clenched and his heart constricted painfully. He ignored the screaming need inside him. Forcing a carefree, unaffected grin—a major feat, considering his body had never been this affected since probably his first time—he looped one of her blonde curls behind her ear, managing to brush the silky shell with his fingertips.

Her sharp intake of breath mirrored the sharp yearning that knifed through his groin. "I'm wrong, remember?"

She blinked. "What?"

If he didn't get out of there, he was going to take her, and to hell with the consequences. "I'm all wrong for you, so you say."

"Yes, but—"

He had to get out of there. He cut her words off with a hand. "If you change your mind, you know the signal."

Turning without another word, he headed down the hallway. He was just getting ready to congratulate himself for his restraint, when her soft voice called out to him. "Rick?"

Without facing her, he managed a gruff, "Yes?"

"Are you going to be home tonight?"

His knees nearly buckled on him.

# Chapter Four

RICK WAS HOME that night, all right. He'd hightailed it out of the office at five, declining Fletch's invitation to grab a cold one at their favorite watering hole.

Restless, nervous energy coursed through him. He leapt in the air and slammed a basketball through the hoop set up in his driveway. Anticipation had built in him all day, and right now he felt on a sky-high adrenaline rush. If Shannon Walsh didn't give him the signal, and soon, he was going to explode.

He didn't want to consider that she might have changed her mind during the day. He'd tried to forestall that possibility by giving her one final mind-altering kiss at the back door that morning. If the strength of her response had been any indication, this day had been a helluva long day for her, as well.

Rick trotted to the ball and scooped it up. Dribbling it, he charged the basket again and slammed the ball home. If Shannon's schedule held true, she'd be home in fifteen minutes. Fifteen interminable minutes, and the real agony would begin.

Bert yelped, and Rick looked to his right. The boy he'd scared out of the tree that morning stood across the street, leaning against a lamp-post, his arms crossed. He scowled at Bert, who'd stopped at the sidewalk and just stood, wagging his tail.

Rick walked toward the kid, the basketball trapped under his arm. "Hey, Tony."

"It's a free country. I can walk down the street if I want to."

Rick stopped at the end of his driveway, cocking his hip and sticking one leg out, mimicking Tony's belligerent stance. His right fist landed on his hip. "You know, Tony, that's what I like about you. Your personality makes you such a pleasure to be around."

"I don't have to be nice to no cops."

"You've got a smart mouth, kid. You got any guts under that skinny little frame to back it up?"

Tony straightened from the lamp-post. His chin hiked up, but a tremor of fear glimmered in his eyes. "I got plenty of guts." He flexed his hands. "Last week I knocked the hell out of Jake Cummins."

"What'd he do?"

Tony cocked his head. "What do you mean?"

"Why'd you knock him around? What'd he do?"

Shrugging, Tony stood tall and puffed out his chest. "Nothing. He was just gettin' on my nerves, is all."

When he was Tony's age, Rick would have considered that as good a reason to fight as any. Luckily he had the benefit of age and experience. He took the ball from under his arm and dribbled it. He'd seen the way Tony's dark eyes kept straying to it, seen the almost wistful look that passed over his features. "Beating the hell out of someone for no reason is not guts, kid. It's sheer stupidity. Guts is when you take a chance on something you care about. You care about anything, Tony?"

"I don't care about nothin'."

"Words to become a loser by."

Tony's eyes followed the bouncing ball with a covetous gleam. "I ain't a loser," he said, almost absent-mindedly.

Rick took the ball and hurtled it at the kid. "Prove it."

Tony caught the ball easily, staring at it as if it were buried treasure. "I don't need to prove nothin' to you, cop."

"The name's Rick. Like that ball?"

"Yeah, it's sweet," Tony said, testing its bounce.

"I'll play you for it."

Tony gaped at him. "Huh?"

"How about a game of horse? You know how to play?"

"'Course."

"Winner keeps the ball."

"You mean it?"

"I don't say anything I don't mean. Come on." Rick turned his back on the kid and walked up the driveway, half-expecting

Tony to take off with his ball. When he heard the bounce of it following him, he allowed himself a slight smile. The kid had potential.

He walked to the foul line he'd measured and painted, then turned to Tony and held out his hands. "Since it's my ball right now, I go first."

Tony scowled, but passed it to him without comment.

Keeping his expression properly serious, Rick set up for the shot, grateful he had something to keep his mind off Shannon Walsh.

Tony's next words shattered that illusion. "You like the babe in the red house, or something?"

Now how did he answer that? Did he like Shannon? He had no idea. He barely knew her. But what he did know about her, he liked a great deal. He shrugged. "Yeah, I guess. She seems nice enough." He hit the shot.

Tony went to the foul line and tossed the ball through the hoop. "Nothin' but net," he crowed, as Rick retrieved it.

Rick set up. Just as he was about to shoot, Tony piped up. "She's a hot babe, huh?"

Missing the shot by a mile, he frowned at Tony. "You plan on going back to that tree?"

"Uh-uh," Tony said, and hit his shot. "That's an 'h' for you."

Just as Rick was about to shoot again, Tony said, "So is she hot, or what?"

Rick stopped himself from shooting. "Are we playing ball or talking about women?"

Tony shrugged. "I just think she's pretty."

Rick told himself it was absurd to be jealous of a kid. "Yeah, she's pretty."

"You got a woman?"

"No. How about you?"

"Nah."

They shot in silence for a while. At this point they both had "HO." Rick kept his gaze on the hoop as he said, casually, "You're pretty good at ball. You on the team at school?"

"Hell, no. That's for sissies."

"Ah, that's bull and you know it. Making the team is an achievement, something to be proud of. And you wouldn't believe how women love a ball player."

He saw uncertainty flash in Tony's eyes. He almost continued the push, but decided to drop the subject for now. The seed had been planted, and he knew that if he made it sound like it was important to him Tony wouldn't even consider the idea. He certainly had the talent, Rick decided, as he watched Tony swish another shot through the bucket.

They played on. When they were both one missed shot from losing, Tony stepped back, about eighteen feet from the basket. He bounced the ball twice, then shot. It hit the backboard, then dropped into the net.

He jumped in the air, his arms raised in victory. When he landed, he smiled at Rick—for one instant, his look was unguarded, happy—then the cocky attitude settled once more on his face.

Rick forced himself to scowl, even while he felt a twinge of pride. The kid had taken a risk, and it had paid off. There was hope for the boy, after all.

Rick set up in the same spot Tony had just shot from. He pretended intense concentration, then shot, making it look good, but not good enough. It bounced off the rim of the net.

Tony whooped, then retrieved the ball. He held it against his chest. His grin vanished. "You made the bet, man."

Rick shrugged. "The ball's yours."

"Really?"

"I said so, didn't I?" He glanced under the scotch pine in his front yard, where Bert lounged. "Stay, Bert."

Bert leapt to his feet and came trotting over. He stopped in front of Tony, who looked just a little frightened.

"He won't hurt you."

Tony patted Bert awkwardly, still clutching the basketball.

Rick checked his watch. Damn, it was seven-thirty. Shannon might have already signaled to him.

He nodded at Tony. "Go on, get out of here. I've got things

to do."

"Can I really keep the ball?"

"On one condition."

Tony frowned. "What?"

"That you come back here some day and let me challenge you to a re-match."

"Not for the ball!"

"No, not for the ball. For the sake of my pride."

Grinning, Tony said, "You won't win. I'm going to practice."

"Big talk for a little kid."

"You'll see." He turned and headed down the driveway, dribbling the entire way. At the sidewalk, he looked back. "You're not too much of a creep for a cop."

"Thanks a lot, kid."


SHANNON PACED back and forth across her living room for a good half-hour. Desire warred with common sense, and common sense was coming out the winner.

Which didn't please her one bit.

She'd had a full day to mull over her options. A full day to anticipate a night of sinful pleasure. Before Rick had left this morning, he'd kissed her and whispered in her ear exactly what he wanted from her, what he wanted to do to her.

And, heaven help her, she wanted it too.

She tried to come up with that list of all the reasons she shouldn't get involved with the man, but the reasons were getting fuzzier in her mind. His health wasn't an issue, after all. He'd had the audacity to enlist Diane's help in that regard. She'd slapped his file on Shannon's desk that morning. The quarterly blood tests Vice cops were required to take were all there. Three weeks ago, Rick tested negative for all STD's and drug use. In addition, he'd even had Diane meet him during her lunch hour and draw his blood. As of four o'clock this afternoon, Rick Hardison tested negative for HIV.

He was disgustingly healthy.

Okay, so she didn't have to worry about disease. And she

certainly didn't have to worry about getting too involved with him. Other than the fact that she found him savagely sexy, he wasn't the type of man she could fall for.

Thank goodness.

No, Shannon wanted an upstanding man, a pillar of the community. If not Mark, someone like him. She wanted a man who would be solid and loving, predictable and dependable.

The only thing solid about Rick was his body. The only thing predictable, his sexual appetite. She felt certain she could depend on him to make love really well, to give her the kind of sexual encounter she knew was possible, but had yet to experience.

She wanted to experience.

God help her, she wanted it badly.

Pushing all doubts from her mind, Shannon resolutely headed down the hallway. In the bathroom, she hesitated only a moment before tearing off her clothes and climbing into the shower.

After scrubbing herself clean, she got out and wrapped a thick terry towel around her. Telling herself she still hadn't made the commitment, she donned peach panties, spritzed herself with perfume, then dressed in a pair of khaki shorts and a paisley vest.

Taking a deep breath, Shannon pulled a brush through her hair while she wandered back down the hall. At the bathroom door, she stopped. And breathed. And held her hand over her erratically beating heart.

It was almost nine-thirty, and the sun had set, darkness settling in over Fairfax, Virginia. Shannon marched into the bathroom and snapped open the blind. Then, her hand trembling, she flicked on the light.

On jellied limbs, she moved out to the living room to wait.

THE SIGNAL.

Rick stared out the window, as he'd been doing on and off for the last ninety minutes. He blinked, wondering if it were a mirage. He now understood how a dehydrated man felt, lost in the desert.

Rubbing his eyes, he looked out again. Shannon's bathroom window blind stayed decidedly open, the light continued to shine.

The signal. Shannon was giving him the signal.

Rick spun from the window and strode across the room. Passing his bed, he picked up the spray of three roses he'd bought that evening on his way home from work. When Bert started to follow him, he stopped. "Sorry, pal, but this is between me and the lady. Come!"

Ears drooping his disappointment, Bert slowly lowered himself to the floor.

As soon as Shannon opened her back door, Rick stepped inside, still not certain about her intent. Her eyes were wide with a sort of frightened curiosity. Rick wanted to chase off the fright and satisfy the curiosity.

He reached behind him and shut the door, its click the only sound in the small kitchen. "Hello."

"H-hi."

"You look . . . great."

That was no lie. She had on a vest, a pair of shorts and not much else. Her slender legs were bare, her toenails painted.

She passed a hand through her mop of hair and laughed, the sound coming out just a little shaky. "Thanks. You too."

Since he wore only jeans and a t-shirt, he knew she was just being polite. "Uh . . . these are for you," he said, handing her the fire red roses.

Her mouth popped open as she stared at the roses. You'd think no man had ever given her any. Now that he thought about it, except for a few formal dances in high school and college, he'd never given a woman flowers before. He wasn't into romantic gestures as a rule. Mary Anne had hated that about him.

Shannon took the flowers, her surprise giving way to a delighted smile that warmed his blood. Maybe there was something to this romantic stuff after all.

As she breathed in the scent of the roses, Rick admired her

bare arms and shoulders. His heated blood thickened in his veins. The anticipation that flowed through him all day, now slowed and hardened into an almost overpowering need.

He took the flowers from her and tossed them on the counter. It was time, past time, for Rick and Shannon to get to know each other.

Dragging her against him, he stared down into those large, luminescent eyes. "Tell me you're not a virgin."

"I'm not a virgin," she whispered.

"Thank God."

Her jaw clicked open. "You're glad about that?"

"Hell yes," he said against her neck. He breathed in her scent. "I didn't want to worry about hurting you."

"You . . . won't hurt me."

Rick bracketed her head and kissed her, the fever in his blood raging. When he finally released her lips, he took a deep breath, searching for control over his fire-ravaged body. "It's time, Shannon. I can't wait for you any longer."

"Do you have protection?"

"Oh, yes."

"And . . . and it'll just be this once."

"Just tonight," he half-agreed. It had to be more than once. He was too hot for her to do her justice the first time around. He needed to at least partially sate this uncontrolled desire before he could fully worship her the way she deserved.

"Because . . . you know, you have long hair."

He picked her up, then grabbed the roses. "True."

"And you wear earrings."

He strode into the living room. "True again."

"And, well, you don't look very respectable."

He headed down her narrow hallway, kicking doors open along the way. "I'm definitely not respectable."

She laid her head on his shoulder. "You . . . don't like to shave much, do you?"

He found what he assumed was her bedroom, and laid her on the bed. "Shannon?"

"Yes?"

"Shut up." And to help her in that endeavor, he covered her mouth with his.

Shannon had been right about one thing, she thought mindlessly. Rick Hardison was a fierce lover, a savage who assaulted her senses until she reeled from the fever pitch of his lovemaking.

No man had ever treated her like this before, like she was his favorite toy, to be greedily hoarded, possessed. He'd torn off her clothes without a thought to buttons and zippers and once she was naked, he'd begun his frenzied lovemaking.

He made raw, guttural noises as he ravished her breasts, suckled her shoulders, her ribs, her belly. While he nipped his way up her legs, he spread her thighs wide, exposing her to his heated gaze, his delicious touch.

Shannon gave herself to him with an abandon that shocked and frightened her. She'd never been so sexually aroused, so needy for a man's touch, his invasion. He reduced her body to a mass of raw, aching nerve endings, and all she could do was accept it, accept him, until she was begging for release from the pressure that threatened to burst and shatter her into a million pieces.

"Please, oh, please," she cried, as his fingers slipped inside her.

He covered her body with his, still using his fingers to stretch her, prepare her for his sex. "So sweet," he rasped, before taking her breast in his mouth.

The double assault undid her. She came apart in his arms. Her muscles clenched and released, as waves of mindless ecstasy crashed through her.

"Rick!" she screamed.

Just as she thought she couldn't take anymore, he plunged his body into hers, and her orgasm began all over again. She threw her head back, clutching at his shoulders and hips. Rick rocked into her slowly, then fast, smoothly, then hard, seeming to know exactly how to wring every ounce of pleasure from her body.

"Open your eyes," he half-gasped, half-growled. "I want to

see it."

Shannon forced her eyes open, gulping for air.

Rick drilled her with his dark gaze. "You are so beautiful." Then he drove into her again, and his own eyes fluttered as his jaw clenched and his throat went taut. "This feels . . . so damn good."

His thrusts became shorter and harder, and Shannon found herself peaking again. This had never happened to her, and she sobbed as the beautiful sensations welled in her again.

Just as she began to come down from the clouds, Rick shoved his hand through her hair and clutched her head. "Shannon!" he whispered against her lips. Then with one final thrust, he buried himself deep inside her, moaned, and his rigid body collapsed.

Shannon welcomed his weight, felt the thundering of his heart, heard the harsh gusts of his breaths. Feeling deliciously languid, she explored the hard planes of his back.

She didn't know how long they laid there, silent, except for the laboring of their lungs. His head was buried in the hollow of her neck.

Shannon wanted to say something, but she didn't know what. "Thank you," seemed a little too polite for two people who'd just engaged in anything but polite sex.

"Wow," seemed more appropriate, but the word stuck in her throat. A sudden terrible fear that she'd never experience lovemaking like that again squeezed at her heart.

There was a wicked side to Shannon that she'd always feared she possessed: she liked hot, raw sex. She had denied it while she'd been involved with Mark. She'd convinced herself that she enjoyed the way he treated her as if she were a priceless piece of china that would break apart if he handled her too roughly. His gentle, sometimes tentative caresses had made her smile, and even, sometimes, find a welcome release.

But Mark had never, ever made her scream.

Sometime later Rick lifted up and propped his head on his hand as he stared down at her. His other hand traced her eyebrows, then pushed back the damp curls near her temples. "I didn't hurt you, did I?"

Her throat closed up. She'd had her fling. It was over now, and all she had left was a memory she'd carry in the most precious part of her soul. She couldn't speak, she felt so suddenly bereft. So she just shook her head.

He smiled. God, he was such a beautiful beast. Dark and hard, he was all sharp angles. She wanted those hard lips to kiss hers again. She wanted them frantically skimming over her flesh.

But he didn't kiss her, not her lips or any other part of her. What he did was disengage their bodies and roll to his side.

Shannon shivered from the abrupt lack of his heat. Was he just going to get up now, get dressed and walk out? How did one end a one-night stand? She hoped he at least knew how to do it nicely. After what had just happened to her, a "Have a nice life, baby," would be devastating. Please, she prayed silently, don't let him make a crude comment.

When he didn't immediately leave the bed, Shannon was heartened a little. Maybe he wouldn't just rush off, now that he'd been sated. She rather liked the idea of cuddling for a while first.

As if he'd read her mind, he pulled her toward him, a slight smile on his lips. His index finger whispered down her nose, to her mouth. He traced its shape. "Wow!" he whispered.

Her heart did cartwheels of joy and laughter bubbled up in her throat. "I couldn't agree more."

"Lady, you are one hot number."

Number, she thought glumly. That's all she was to him was a number. Her smile and her joy vanished. "And just which number would I be?" she asked, then regretted it as he frowned. After all, she had no right to question him that way.

"I wouldn't know," he said, his words clipped. "I don't cut notches."

"I'm sorry," she whispered, running her palm over his bristly jaw. "I had no right to ask."

He threaded his fingers through her hair, seemingly fascinated with the jumbled mess. "Hey, curiosity's not a bad thing. Especially in a scientist."

She could have told him that it wasn't curiosity that had

prompted the question, but a sudden urge to be more than just another faceless fling. She didn't. After all, that's all they could ever be to each other. Anything more would be just plain stupid. Rick Hardison was not the type of man one brought home to meet mother and father.

Several silky, ink-black strands of his hair had come loose from the leather thong holding it back. She wanted to unloose all of his hair, but that wouldn't be nice since he was leaving anytime now.

"What are you thinking, Shannon?" he asked her.

"I . . . was thinking that you have long hair."

He seemed to go stiff. "Yes, I know, it's a real drawback."

"Actually," she said quickly, to mollify him, "I was thinking that I'd like to take it out of the ponytail."

His eyebrows shot up. "Well then, go ahead."

"But . . . aren't you leaving now?"

"Is that what you want?" he asked, his tone guarded.

"Uh, well, I don't know. I've never done this before."

"Do you want me to go, Shannon?" he asked again. "Because if you do, I will."

"What . . . what would happen if you stayed a while?"

He grinned. Then he reached across her body for something. When he laid back, he had one of the roses in his hand. He wisped it across her forehead, then down her nose. He traced her lips, then skimmed it down her chin and throat.

The rose circled her breast languidly, and Shannon's body responded like a flash fire. She sucked in her breath.

"This," he said, "This would happen."

"Stay," Shannon breathed, as the rose whispered between her legs.

"WELL?" DIANE asked Shannon, first thing the next morning. She plopped down in the chair beside Shannon's steel desk, her brown eyes twinkling with curiosity.

Shannon clicked off the machine she'd been dictating a report into and sat back. "Well, what?"

"Tell me everything."

Tapping her pencil on her handwritten notes, Shannon said, "All the blood swatches test consistent with the victim. None test consistent with—"

"Shannon . . ."

She raised a brow, but her heart leapt. She knew exactly what information Diane was digging for. Where she came from, women didn't even acknowledge they'd been intimate with a man, much less tell each other details. But Fairfax, Virginia was a different planet from Belleville, Pennsylvania. And Diane Mackenzie was a different species from her girlfriends back home.

Besides, Shannon was confused. She welcomed the advice of a woman more experienced in matters such as these. "Yes, it happened."

"Really?" Diane squealed. She lowered her voice. "Was he as good as his reputation?"

Shannon sniffed. "I wouldn't know what his reputation is, but . . . well—"

"Was he good?"

"Oh, Diane," Shannon cried softly. "He was wonderful."

Diane smacked the table. "I knew it."

A dam broke inside Shannon. "He was wild and sweet and rough and gentle and I feel right now like I survived a tornado. Every single muscle I own is sore."

"Sore is good."

"Yes, it is," Shannon agreed, her voice soft and wistful.

Diane peered at her. "If it was so good, why do you look like you're contemplating a good cry?"

Shannon bit her lip. "It's over."

"Over? Why?"

"It was just a one-night stand, Diane. We both agreed to that. I mean, at first I thought that meant just one time, period. Well, it turned out to be many more times than one, but still, the night is over. We're finished, done, kaput."

"Did he tell you that?"

"Not exactly. It's just that we both went into it with open eyes. One night. That's all he wanted, all I wanted. He got what he wanted from me. Now it's on to his next conquest."

Steepling her fingers, Diane said, studying her nails, "So, did he scratch your itch? Are you over the fling fantasy?"

"He scratched it all right. But somehow it's turned into poison ivy. The more he scratched, the more I itched."

"So, you're still itching for him, is that it?"

"Yes!" Shannon nearly wailed.

"This is not a problem."

"Why not?" Shannon asked, feeling her eyes light with hope.

"It's a good bet that if you're still itchy, so's he."

"How do you know?"

"I just know men. If you're still hot for him, it's a good bet he's still hot for you."

"Do you—" Shannon shook her head. "No, I don't think so. He's the type of man who takes then moves on." She sighed. "Besides, even if we clicked in the bedroom, we're still all wrong for each other."

Diane patted her arm. "Take my advice. Go to his house tonight. My bet is your one night can easily be stretched into two."


RICK OPENED his front door, and saw the object of his fantasy standing there, looking beautiful and frightened. He'd thought of nothing but Shannon all day, wondering how he was going to find a way to see her again. The last thing he expected was for her to come to his home.

"Shannon," he kind of choked. "Come in."

She appeared so nervous, he wondered if something had happened. Was she worried she was pregnant? None of the condoms had broken. Besides, it was a little early for her to be worrying that a stray sperm had slipped past.

He stepped back, and she hesitated, looking like a jittery rabbit. Then she moved into the house and peered around.

Her fear seemed to leave her momentarily, as she gazed at the mess. So he wasn't a great housekeeper. Big deal.

Bert came running in and immediately greeted Shannon

with an ecstatic woof. Shannon knelt and scratched him, making him one happy puppy.

Rick was too much of a cynic to hope that she was there for the same reason he wanted her to be there. God, he'd wracked his brain all day, wondering how to get her to let him crawl into her bed again and let him play with that fantasy body one more time.

Shannon stood and gave him a trembly smile. Rick waited, every muscle in him tense.

Finally she blurted, "I'm still itchy."

"Excuse me?"

"I . . . still have the itch, and Diane said that if I do, you might too. So I thought I'd see if maybe you'd agree that one more night couldn't hurt." She started to turn back to the door. "But, I think I made a big mistake—"

He grabbed her wrist and turned her back to him. "I'm still itchy, too."

"Really?"

"Oh, yeah. It's eating me up."

"So, one more night couldn't hurt, right?"

"No, one more couldn't hurt."

"Just one though, because we're all wrong for each other."

"All wrong," he agreed, picking her up and heading for the staircase.

"It's just sex."

"That's all it is."

"All it can ever be."

"Right."

He took the steps two at a time.

"An itch."

"Shannon?"

"I know, I know. Shut up."

# Chapter Five

TWO WEEKS LATER, Rick was still itchy. He fell onto Shannon's lush, naked body, panting, exhausted, but definitely not sated. At least not in the sense that he'd had his fill of her. In fact, the more he had her, the more he wanted her.

The more he wanted from her.

This was a first for him. He didn't consider it a particularly honorable character trait of his, but he'd always grown bored fairly fast with the women he dated. With Shannon it was different. He not only wasn't bored, he was actually curious. In two weeks, they'd slept together almost every night, but he still knew close to nothing about her. She didn't show any interest in sharing personal details about herself.

And strangely enough, that was beginning to bother him.

He raised up on his forearms and gazed down at her. Something in his chest lurched at the glittering, satisfied smile on her face. No doubt about it, she loved sex. Any and every kind of sex.

Rick grinned slowly. "You're incredible, you know that?"

She gave a throaty chuckle. "I'm glad you think so. Likewise."

He bent and took her breast in his mouth, their lower bodies still joined. She arched up, fairly purring. Their biggest problem in two weeks was having to take the time to change condoms between acts of lovemaking. If not for that inconvenience, Rick felt certain he'd never leave the tight, milking heat of her. The moment he'd finish climaxing, his desire would begin to build all over again. She made him insatiable.

Her fingers threaded through his hair, and she held his

mouth against her breast. Her gasps of delight made him feverish to possess her again, to find sweet, sweet release inside her.

But he had practical matters to take care of first. Reluctantly he lifted his lips from her breast and rolled off of her. While he cleaned himself up, some rational side of his mind returned, and he realized he didn't just want to take her again. For the first time in his life, he wanted to talk to a woman more than have sex with her.

When he didn't replace the condom, a sound of protest clicked in her throat. She looked at him strangely as he laid down beside her and pulled her into his arms. She settled comfortably in the crook of his shoulder, and Rick smiled down at her mop of curls, tickling the skin of his arm.

He kissed her temple, then trailed his fingertips over her face. For an incredibly sexy, passionate woman, she had deceptively angelic features. Right now she looked like a pure, untouched virgin.

Except for the fact that she was unabashedly naked.

He liked that about her too. She had a fantastic body, she knew he thought so, and she used it to entice him in ways that made him wild, primal.

The combination of innocence in her eyes and wanton lust in her hands, her body, had him crazy. He thought about her constantly, counted the minutes until he could rush to her home and capture her lips, strip her naked, and send them both hurtling headlong into mindless bliss.

Her wide eyes turned up to look at him and she smiled her pleasure as his fingers stroked over her satiny skin. He didn't think he'd ever get tired of touching her.

"What are you thinking right now?" he asked her.

She sighed. "That what you're doing feels good."

He kissed her temple, whispering against her curls, "Good. I like making you feel good."

Her lips curved sweetly. "I've noticed."

His fingers traveled down to her shoulder. "Tell me about your family."

Her gaze jerked to his, and a wariness slipped into the depths of her eyes. "Why?"

"I'm just interested. It occurs to me I don't know anything about you."

She hesitated. "You know what's important."

His fingers stilled. "I know what's important?"

"Yes."

"What's that?"

"You know . . . you know how to . . . make me . . . feel good."

He chuckled, but it felt and sounded forced. Probably because it was. "I see."

She struggled out of his arms and pulled a sheet up around her. The sudden modesty irritated him, like she wanted to hide from him.

"I mean," she said quickly, apparently recognizing something wrong in his face, in his immediately tense body, "it's not like we're dating."

"Oh?" he asked in a bland, bored voice. He felt anything but bland or bored, but he didn't understand what he did feel, so he feigned nonchalance. "What are we doing?"

She emitted a nervous puff of laughter. "Why, we're . . . having an affair."

"So that means we're not allowed to get to know each other?"

"I'm thirsty. Want something to drink?"

"No."

She jumped out of bed and threw on her robe. "Well, I think I'll just get myself a soda."

Rick kicked at the jumbled sheets and stood up, stalking naked through the house to the kitchen. He found her pouring a Coke over ice.

"You didn't answer my question."

She looked up, eyes wide. "Oh! You startled me."

"Sorry. Answer the question, Shannon."

"I . . . think I've forgotten it."

Like hell, Rick thought, his irritation rising rapidly. "I'd like to understand the rules here, sweetheart. What you're saying is, since this is just about sex, our minds, our personal lives, are off-limits?"

She took a long sip. A stall tactic if he'd ever seen one. After wiping her mouth with a paper towel, she said, "Don't you think it's better that way? Less complications when it's . . . over."

"Telling me where you're from, about your family, will make things complicated?"

"Yes."

"Why?"

"It just . . . will."

"Fine." Not quite sure why he was angry, Rick spun on his heel and stomped out of the kitchen.

"Rick?" Shannon called after him. Then he heard her racing behind him, trying to catch up.

His strides grew longer. He headed into the bedroom, swiped his jeans from the floor and yanked out his briefs. Shoving them on, he refused to look up, even though he knew she was standing there.

"You're leaving?"

"Yes."

"Why?"

While he tugged on his jeans, he answered her. "Maybe I'm getting tired of a one-dimensional relationship."

He heard her take a sharp breath. "You're tired? Of me?"

He gave up trying to zip his jeans. Looking up, he saw the hurt in her eyes. Now why would she feel hurt? She just all but admitted that she wasn't interested in anything about him, save his body. And she was feeling hurt?

Well, at least she'd been honest about it. She'd never pretended she wanted anything but a sexual relationship with him. And up until now he'd been quite content with that arrangement. Hell, he'd been on cloud nine. Not many men got this kind of opportunity to indulge their baser needs as much as they wanted without having to offer a piece of their souls in return.

Yanking his t-shirt over his head, he questioned his sanity.

Why was he angry? He was getting absolutely everything he wanted from her. And nothing he didn't want.

But right now, he felt used. Why that bothered him, he couldn't say. But it did. "No, I'm not tired of you, Shannon. Maybe I'm just not in the mood for sex right now. And since that's what this . . . affair is limited to, there's not much reason for me to stay, is there?"

She strolled over to him and smoothed her palms over his ribs. "I bet I can change your mind."

He knew she could change his mind. Which for some reason made him even angrier. Suddenly, feeling like a sex machine didn't appeal to him. Taking her hands from his body, he set her away from him. "I'm not in the mood to have my mind changed."

Before he relented in the face of her hurt and astonishment, he walked past her out the bedroom door. As he headed down the hallway, he buckled his belt.

"Are . . . are you ever coming back?" Shannon asked, as he put his hand on the back door knob.

He couldn't look at her. "I don't know."

"Oh."

"Goodbye, Shannon."

He got no answer.


IN THE END, he'd lasted two days before he'd returned to Shannon. He'd gone through several mutations of feelings in that time. Finally he'd decided he was cutting off his nose to spite his face. Why deny himself?

It was now exactly one month since their "one-night stand" had begun. Rick felt this really stupid desire to celebrate their anniversary. He'd even gone so far the other evening as to ask Shannon if she wanted to go out to dinner tonight. She'd looked at him with those wide eyes and shaken her head till he thought it'd unscrew off her neck.

As he bounced the basketball to Tony, Rick frowned. He had the feeling that her reluctance to go out with him on a "date" didn't stem only from her fear of turning this into a normal relationship. He had the feeling she was actually ashamed of him. She didn't want to be seen in his company.

Shannon had learned every secret his body possessed over the last several weeks, but she still knew nothing about his mind. And that fact was starting to get on his nerves again. She didn't want to see past the man with the long hair and earring, and she certainly didn't want the public to know she associated with him.

Which made him want to tell her to go to hell.

So why couldn't he?

He understood why she wanted to keep an emotional distance. It would be easier for both of them when the fire in their physical relationship died and they went their separate ways. Still, little things about Shannon had made themselves known to him, and, unfortunately, he liked what he'd learned—even as he realized that she didn't consider him respectable lover material in the eyes of her world.

One night she'd surprised him by challenging him to a game of strip Trivial Pursuit. While the game hadn't lasted long, because the erotic unveiling of their bodies had overcome them, they'd played long enough for Rick to discover that Shannon was surprisingly knowledgeable about more subjects than science. And that she had a sense of humor underneath that irresistible face of hers.

He'd had to fight the desire to ask her what her hobbies were, what interested her. As far as she was concerned, he didn't need to know any of that. As far as she was concerned, he knew all that he needed to know. He knew how she liked to make love.

"Man, you suck today, cop," Tony sneered, as Rick let him run right by him and hook in a shot.

Rick shook his head, then "oomphed!" when Tony hurled the ball at his gut. He found himself distracted a lot, lately. Even Fletch had noticed and complained about it. And Fletch had a good point. In their line of work, allowing himself to get distracted by the thought of big blue eyes and soft, pliant lips could prove deadly.

Rick swore under his breath, then moved to the foul line,

dribbling the basketball. If he had any brains, he'd break off this thing with Shannon already, and find himself another lover, one who wouldn't make him want to explore her soul.

"C'mon, man," Tony complained. "This has to be the lamest game of one-on-one I ever played."

Irritated with himself, Rick charged Tony, then veered at the last second and sank a bank shot. "Stick that in your ear, kid."

"Finally!" Tony retorted. "Where were you just now? On Mars?"

More like on Maple. "I was just thinking. Had to bust a kid your age today. Really made me sick."

He'd been meaning to bring up the subject of gangs to Tony on several occasions, but hadn't known how to broach the topic. The bust that day at Tony's school provided a good excuse.

Tony snorted. "Raleigh Walker's a total bonehead."

"You know the kid?"

"Yeah." Tony easily shot over Rick's head.

"You two friends?"

"Nah. He's a Crow. They're all a bunch of weasels."

"What do you think of the Eagles?" Rick asked, referring to the rival gang.

"They're all right," Tony said, passing him the ball.

"You're not thinking of joining them, are you?" Rick asked bluntly.

Tony shrugged and retrieved the ball, tossing it to Rick.

"Was that a 'yes' or a 'no?'"

Tony shrugged again. "Not really."

"Not really? What kind of answer is that? That's like saying your girlfriend's not really pregnant. Are you or aren't you? It's a simple question."

"What, you gonna bust my chops if I say yes?"

Rick let the ball drop to the ground, whistled to Bert and started walking toward his front door.

"Where you going?"

"I don't waste my time with idiots." He turned back to the

kid. "You know, I feel sorry for you, Tony. You've got a real talent for basketball. You could use it, let it help you get a college education. Instead, you join a gang and you're on a fast-track to no-freaking-where. God, how stupid."

"What the hell do you care?" Tony shouted. "Don't tell me you ain't never been in a gang."

Rick clenched his teeth. Truth or fiction? This kid reminded him so much of himself as a teenager, it sometimes hurt just to look at him. And he knew that at Tony's age, he wouldn't have listened to the Voice of Experience. It had taken drastic measures by his grandfather and a harsh awakening by a police officer to get him to open his eyes.

Still, Tony deserved the truth. "Yes, I was once in a gang," he admitted quietly.

Tony's eyes flashed in triumph. "So who are you to be telling me what to do?"

Rick stalked back to Tony and hauled him up by his t-shirt. "I'll tell you who I am. I'm the guy who lost both my parents—such as they were—to gang violence. I was younger than you are at the time. I'm the guy who for three years roamed the streets and back alleys, beating the hell out of any rival gang member who was unlucky enough to stumble into my path. I landed in juvie hall. I broke out of juvie hall. So when they caught up with me again, they put me in a regular prison. You wouldn't like a regular prison, Tony. You wouldn't like it at all. But that's just where you're going to end up if you don't clean up your act."

"I'm not going to no prison!" Tony shouted. "I can't! Coach says if I want to make the team this year, I can't be part of that scene."

Rick dropped Tony's shirt. "You're going out for the team?"

"Maybe," Tony mumbled, rubbing his chest.

Rick slapped him on the shoulder. "All right!" He was shocked, really. Tony hadn't brought up the subject once since Rick had first mentioned it weeks ago. Rick had assumed Tony had forgotten all about it. "That's great! I can't wait to come watch you play."

Tony's eyes rounded. "You'd come watch?"

"Hell, yes! And cheer pretty loud, too, I'd imagine."

Tony stared at him, then his sullen expression returned. "You're just saying that."

"Tony, if you go out for the team and make it, I promise I'll come to as many of your games as is humanly possible. I swear it."

"Yeah, you and my old man."

Ahhh, here we go. "What about your old man?"

"He says he'll come too, but I know he won't. He doesn't give a damn what I do."

"I bet you're dead wrong about that."

"You don't know my old man." He shrugged as if it didn't matter to him. "All he cares about is his damn job. He doesn't care about us at all."

Rick was intimately aware of how it felt to have a father who put something before his family. Jobs, pills, booze, gambling, it didn't matter what. Knowing you played second fiddle to some other entity hurt. In his case, that other entity had been his father himself. He'd been the most selfish, self-absorbed bastard Rick had ever known. His mother had been just as bad.

"I'll be there, Tony. I promise I'll be there." Rick shamelessly appealed to Tony's sense of greed. "I'll give you fifty bucks if I'm not at your first game."

"Cool!"

"And a hundred bucks at the end of the season if I don't make it to more than half the home games."

"Cool!"

They high-fived to seal the deal. Then Rick stole the ball from Tony's hands and ran around him, slamming it through the hoop.

SHANNON SHOULDN'T have eavesdropped on the conversation.

She didn't want or need to know that Rick Hardison would

try anything, including bribery, to help out a troubled teenage boy. She didn't want to know that he'd overcome horrendous tragedy in his childhood. She didn't want to consider that he'd chosen his profession consciously, that he didn't just happen to become a Vice cop.

God, this was terrible. She'd spent a month making certain she learned as little as possible about Rick. It was for the best, she'd reasoned, considering any night might be their last.

Shannon had carefully split her life in two. On one side was the here and now Shannon. On the other was the Shannon working for long term. There was no room on the long term side for intimate details about Rick. He belonged completely on the side of here and now.

And knowing that he was a caring, giving human being somehow blurred that line.

Shannon watched Rick steal the ball from the boy's hand and sail around him to dunk it through the basket. She admired his masculine grace with what she hoped was detached appreciation. Yes, indeed, Shannon's lover of the moment was one sexy hunk.

Rick turned back to the boy, Tony, with a grin. He started to say something, then stopped and looked at Shannon. That's when Shannon realized that the boy stood gaping at her, and Rick had merely followed his gaze.

She flushed. Rick had mentioned this boy in passing a couple of times, but he'd never told her he was acting as a sort of big brother to him. It made her heart lurch a little, which she considered a very dangerous reaction.

"I . . . I'm sorry, I didn't mean to interrupt."

At the sound of her voice, Har—Rick's dog looked up from whatever small bug he'd been tormenting, and barked, then bounded over to her.

She felt like a fool. She'd been daydreaming about Rick all afternoon, and she'd come straight to his house from work, intent on seducing him if he were home. Not that she'd have to work hard. Rick Hardison had to be the most easily seducible man on planet earth. She could do it with a smile, a touch, the breathy use of his name.

She couldn't do it with a teenage boy gawking at her.

Rick walked to her, smiling that dark, sexy smile that—in a very tiny corner of her heart—she hoped he reserved for her.

"Nice surprise," he said when he reached her. He lowered his voice. "I was about to come see you."

He turned back to the boy. "Tony, close your mouth and come over here. I don't think you've met Shannon close up, have you?"

*Met me close up? What's that supposed to mean?*

The boy's face turned crimson, but he finally—albeit reluctantly—shuffled over to them. "'Lo," he mumbled.

"Hello, Tony. Nice to meet you."

"Yeah."

"Nice to meet you as well, Shannon," Rick instructed.

"Nice to meetcha," Tony conceded.

"You're very good at basketball," Shannon told him, which made him flush even redder.

"Tony just mentioned he's going out for the school team this year," Rick said, his pride evident.

Tony squirmed, but then looked up at Rick, and if Shannon had ever wanted to capture a picture of what hero-worship looked like, she should have snapped a Polaroid at that very moment.

Shannon didn't want to know that someone hero-worshipped Rick. That line she'd drawn in her life was starting to wobble before her very eyes. She had to get out of there. No matter how much she'd wanted to make love with Rick tonight, things were too shaky in her head right now. She couldn't think clearly enough to just enjoy the sex.

"Well, I just stopped by to say hi," she said brightly. "You two get back to your game."

"Don't leave," Rick pleaded in a low growl. One that made her aware of every nerve ending in her, right down to her toenails.

"I . . . really have to," she said, fervently meaning it. "Well, hope to see you again some time, Tony."

Rick shot her a puzzled frown and opened his mouth to protest, but she whirled before he had a chance and practically ran to her car.

"WHY THE HELL'D you leave?" Rick asked her, the moment she opened the door. She hadn't been home twenty minutes.

God, he looked gorgeous. He still wore a gray sweatshirt with the sleeves cut out, and his biceps rippled as he crossed his arms. He had on black trunks, so his legs were bare down to his sweat socks and sneakers. His hair was loose, the way she was beginning to like it.

Too much.

Shannon panicked. Her carefully constructed life was crumbling around her ears. When had she started to care about him? That just couldn't happen. It just couldn't.

"Rick, our . . . our affair's over."

Disbelief and something else sparkled in his eyes. "Why?" he asked, in a low, raw voice.

"I'm just . . . " She swallowed. God forgive her for lying. " . . . bored. It was fun, really, but I think it's time for both of us to move on."

He stared at her, unblinking. His body was tense. He looked coiled, ready to pounce. "You didn't seem bored last night."

Oh, God, she'd been far from bored. The thought of never having that again sliced her heart to ribbons. Still, it had to happen, sooner or later. It might as well be sooner, so she could get the grieving process over with and get on with her life. "It's not the sex, Rick. It's the . . . relationship. I'm ready to . . . move on and . . . and find someone who . . . will be a more permanent part of my . . . life."

"And that can't be me, right?"

If he didn't leave, she was going to start bawling. "Please don't make this hard. We both knew it was temporary."

"Why can't it be me?"

"Oh, Rick!" she gasped. "There's just so much . . . you don't understand."

"Make me understand. I deserve that much."

She opened her mouth, closed it, then tried again. Nothing came out.

"Is it how I've treated you? I know I get carried away, I know sometimes I lose control with you, but you always seemed . . . happy, so I thought—"

"No! You've been . . . wonderful."

"Then what, Shannon? What did I do wrong?"

Her chin dropped to her chest and her eyes welled. She'd never felt more like a coward in her life. "It's not you, Rick. It's me. I've never done anything like we've done the last few weeks. I guess it's just getting to me. I was . . . brought up this certain way, and I've broken every rule I know with you. The guilt is . . . getting to me."

His fingers gripped her chin and he forced her head up. "All of a sudden you feel guilty?"

She managed to meet his eyes. "Yes. There's no future for us. I don't want to . . . feel anything for you. And I'm scared if I keep seeing you—"

"Sleeping with me," he interrupted, his jaw taut with anger. "You haven't *seen* me at all."

Shannon couldn't blame him for being angry. She was botching this, just like she botched everything. "Sleeping with you," she agreed softly. "If I keep sleeping with you . . . well, it would hurt."

"Because heaven forbid you feel something for me."

"I can't, Rick," she said, though her heart was giving her fits. "We're not meant for long term. So let's just end it now. Let's make it easier for both of us."

The calm that settled over his features frightened her. She quaked inside and mentally steeled herself for whatever punishment he decided to dish out. Then he smiled, a cold bitter smile that froze her right down to her marrow. "Thanks for the couple hundred lays," he said, then turned on his heel and walked away.

Shannon collapsed against the door frame, feeling like someone had just ripped out her heart. She slammed the door shut before she gave into the monumental urge to beg him to come back.

"WHAT THE HELL'S the matter with you?" Fletch asked Rick, as they sat in the donut shop. Rick was working on his second jelly-fill, while Fletch merely sipped coffee.

"You've been about as fun to work with lately as Attila the Hun," Fletch added. Then he glanced at the donut in Rick's hand and shook his head. "You're becoming a cliché, right before my very eyes. What is your problem?"

Rick bristled. It had been four days since his last conversation with Shannon, and he was in a murdering mood. He swallowed some coffee before answering, "None of your damn business."

"Ah," Fletch said in an omniscient tone. "A woman."

"Wrong," Rick lied.

"Hardison, you might think you're a stoic SOB, but I know you all too well. The last time you were in this foul a mood was the nine months, four days and sixteen hours you were married to Mary Anne. Is it the neighbor broad you mentioned occasionally?"

"Shut up, Fletch."

"It's the neighbor."

Rick didn't rise to the bait.

"What'd she do?"

Rick pressed his lips together.

"She dump you?"

"Kiss ass."

"She dumped you. Why?"

"Because I don't fit her image of a forever kind of guy," Rick said tightly.

Fletch choked on his coffee. "So? The lady's right. You aren't a forever kind of guy."

"I know that!" Rick snapped, then took a steadying breath. "I just wasn't expecting it to be over so soon."

"So soon?" Fletch snorted. "This is the longest running

affair you've had in your life." He peered at Rick closely, making Rick want to squirm. "Don't tell me you fell for her."

"Of course not! Who'd be dumb enough to fall for a woman superficial enough to judge a man by his looks?"

"Your looks?" Fletch laughed. "You know, I've always thought you were an ugly sonofabitch, myself, but the ladies aren't as discerning as me. What in particular did she find wrong with your looks?"

"She thinks I look like a thug."

"Well, I can't argue with that."

Rick scowled at Fletch, who was as squeaky-clean looking as a prep school graduate. Which was why he was always the behind-the-scenes guy. His perfectly cut and combed mahogany brown hair and his penchant to wear tweed didn't exactly inspire confidence in drug dealers and whores.

Shannon would love Fletch.

Shannon. Something vise-like squeezed in his chest whenever he thought about her. He couldn't understand why he even bothered to think about her. He should be glad their affair was over. After all, as she'd told him too many times to count, they were all wrong for each other.

So why couldn't he get her out of his mind, out of his system? It wasn't like he was in love with her, or anything. He didn't even know if he liked her, considering she'd never let him get to know her.

Maybe that was the problem. If he'd gotten to know her, the real her, he would have found plenty of reasons not to like her. Then the sudden lack of sex in his life wouldn't feel so damn painful. There wouldn't be a gnawing hole in the pit of his stomach. He'd be able to sleep. He'd be able to eat. He'd be able to stop fantasizing about her during the day, and dreaming about her during the nights he succeeded at falling into an exhausted sleep.

"You need to get laid, buddy boy."

"Yeah," Rick managed, but with no enthusiasm whatsoever.

He stared out the window, seeing little. Feeling too much.

His life hadn't felt this out of control in many, many years. Another good reason to resent the hell out of Shannon Walsh.

"Hardison, look," Fletch said, jerking him out of his musings. "Appears our hardened felon is back out on the streets."

Rick focused, gazing across the boulevard in the direction Fletch pointed. He managed a wan grin. Mrs. Sugarbaker was scurrying down the sidewalk in a hot pink dress and sturdy black shoes. A black purse hung from her raised forearm. "How much hot cash you think she's carting in that purse?"

Fletch grinned. "Probably enough to buy a small country."

Just then a young man wearing the trademark red bandanna of the Crows came barreling down the street, straight toward the elderly woman. He didn't even slow down as he passed her, but she spun around violently as he yanked her purse from her arm. Rick jumped to his feet and took off, Fletch on his heels.

As he emerged from the donut shop, he heard Mrs. Sugarbaker's indignant squalls and saw her jumping up and down and pointing at the perp.

Rick nearly got hit by a pick-up as he took off after the purse-snatcher. Jumping back out of the way, he lost sight of the kid for a moment, but when the truck passed, he spotted the red bandanna just as the thief veered down an alley. Rick followed, seeing immediately the young man's mistake. The alley was a dead end, with a high concrete wall making the boy's escape impossible.

Rick flashed his badge as he slowed to a walk. "Police, sport. You really shouldn't be committing crimes in front of a donut shop. That's s-t-o-o-p-i-d."

The kid looked terrified, trapped like a deer in the crosshairs.

"Stealing from little old ladies is a real honorable profession, kid," Rick said, stuffing his badge into his back pocket. "What's next? Rolling winos?"

In a surprisingly swift move, the young thug dropped Mrs. Sugarbaker's purse and whipped out a small .22 caliber pistol.

Rick snorted. "Put the damn gun away, you stupid moron."

"Get away!" the kid said, never taking his eyes, or his gun sight from Rick. "Get back."

"Give me the gun, kid," Rick said, slowing, but not stopping his approach. "You shoot me and you're a dead man. My partner's right behind me, and he's rather fond of me. And his gun's a whole lot nastier looking than that cheap little thing you're carting around. It'll blow a hole in you the size of West Virginia."

His threats had no effect on the kid whatsoever. Impatient and in a very foul mood, Rick swiped at the gun. He underestimated the speed of the kid. The boy jumped back, raised the gun, and shot him.

Rick clutched at his shoulder as he heard Fletch shout. In horror he watched the thug-in-training turn the gun toward Fletch. Rick tried to draw his weapon, but his right arm wasn't cooperating. In desperation he launched himself at the kid, the two of them hit the pavement in a bone-jarring thud. The gun flew through the air, but Rick had no idea where it landed. He tried to stand, but only made it to his knees. It took a moment for the pain to hit him. While he waited, he heard Fletch bark, "Freeze!" and then come running over and quickly placing the kid in cuffs, around a fire escape pole so he couldn't get away.

Rick tried again to rise to his feet, but the pain chose that moment to slam into him. He couldn't catch his breath, which made him worried that the bullet might have hit a lung.

Big black spots started sprouting before his eyes, and he had a tough time seeing Fletch. He vaguely heard Fletch's voice, but he couldn't assimilate the words into meaningful dialogue. The raw, burning pain overwhelmed him, and he let some disembodied hands push him to the ground.

"Remind me . . . to give up donuts," Rick rasped.

"Shut up, you fool," Fletch growled, looming over him, as shouts sounded in the far, far distance. Blessed dark was descending on him. Relief. From pain. From life.

Life! Oh, God, life.

Clawing his way back to consciousness, he clutched at the man above him. "Fletch?"

"Yeah, buddy. Just lie still. Help's coming."

Rick bucked when a burning pressure was applied to his shoulder. "Fletch?"

"Relax, dammit!"

"Shannon," he gasped, around the radiating pain. "I . . . need . . . Shannon."

"Shannon who? What's her last name?"

"Walth . . . Welth . . . " His tongue was thick, and Lord he was thirsty. "Crime . . . lab."

"ANYONE EVER TELL you you're just pure joy to work with lately?" Diane asked Shannon.

"I didn't know a cheerful disposition was part of the job description," Shannon retorted, then immediately felt bad. She knew she'd been a real downer in the last four days, but she couldn't seem to shake her melancholy. Yesterday, Diane had pulled her aside and said, "Please, for all of our sakes, go see Rick and jump his bones."

Shannon hadn't been able to bring herself to be that forward, but after an hour of deliberation, she'd opened her bathroom blind and turned on the light. She'd waited four hours, and Rick had never come.

It really was over.

Why that had made her cry deep into the night, she didn't want to guess. She should be glad. She was determined to be glad. Only she couldn't quite pull it off.

"I'm sorry, Diane. I'm sorry for taking it out on you."

Diane sat down and looked at her with concern. "Has it occurred to you that you might have felt a little more for him than just lust?"

"No!" Shannon nearly shouted. "No, that's not possible."

"Why not? Rick's a helluva guy. He's sexy as sin. You could do lots, lots worse."

"I know, it's just . . . oh, hell, Diane. I've had this image in my head all my life of what my mate would be like. Rick just doesn't fit it."

"Hearts don't always listen to images."

Shaking her head, Shannon blinked back tears. "You know what's funny?"

"What?"

"All of my life, I've done the right thing. I've always lived with the knowledge that as the only daughter of a small town preacher, I had a standard to uphold. It's never bothered me. I liked making my parents happy and proud of me. And now I understand why it was so important to them that I had a strong moral base. Because the moment I forgot that—that one moment when I made the decision to get involved with Rick—I was doomed to get burned." She gave a brittle little choking laugh. "I definitely believe the line about paying for your sins."

"What's the sin, Shannon? Having an affair with Rick, or falling for him?"

Shannon stared at her friend, speechless. She hadn't fallen for Rick. Oh, she was madly attracted to him, but that was all. Any more than that would be emotional suicide.

Her phone rang, and she picked it up, grateful for a diversion from the unsettling topic of Rick Hardison and the feelings he invoked deep inside her. "Shannon Walsh."

"Ms. Walsh, my name is Tom Fletcher."

The name meant nothing to her. "Yes?"

"I'm Rick Hardison's partner."

That name meant too much to her. A sense of dread filled her. "Something's happened to Rick," she said, with deadly certainty.

"Yes . . . he's been shot."

Her heart splintered. "No!"

"I'm sorry to have to tell you—"

"He's not dead!"

"No, he's not . . . at least, he wasn't when they wheeled him into surgery. The medics said they didn't think the wound was fatal, though he lost a lot of blood."

"I'm on my way. Fairfax Hospital?"

"Yes. There's really no hurry. They said it would be a while—"

"I'm on my way."

"Fine."

"Don't let them let him die," she whispered, knowing it was a stupid thing to say.

"He's a stubborn SOB, Shannon. He won't die."

"How . . . " She tried to swallow the grapefruit size lump in her throat. "How did . . . you know . . . to call me?"

"He asked for you, right before he passed out."

# Chapter Six

TOM FLETCHER was as solid as an oak tree, and in the hours they waited for word of Rick's condition, Shannon leaned on him, accepting his quiet strength gratefully.

He brought her water, which she forced down her closed throat. He brought her a candy bar, which she refused with a silent shake of her head.

Shannon paced. She cried. She begged God like she'd never begged him before. And through it all, she leaned on Tom Fletcher.

"What's taking so long?" she asked him, for about the tenth time. "If the wound isn't potentially fatal, why would it take this long?"

Tom rubbed his temples, and her concern was mirrored in his eyes. "I don't know. Right now I'm trying to consider no news good news."

"I wish I shared that sentiment."

He managed a reassuring smile, which did nothing to reassure her. "Relax. The man's a bear. And an ornery one at that. He's not going out without a fight."

Absently, Shannon noticed how handsome Tom was. Tall and lean, he had that All-American look about him. He could be the epitome of her life-long dream man. But though she found him very attractive, he didn't do a thing for her.

His rich, brown hair was cropped short and neat. A very nice style. But then, when he was kissing a woman's body, she wouldn't know the joy, the pleasure of his long locks tickling, sensitizing her skin.

Tom's eyes were a lovely hazel, more green than brown, and they sparkled in a very charming way. Still, she didn't find them as compelling as sable eyes could be, when they stared into hers with a passion, a heat that made her blood simmer.

He was as tall, if not taller than Rick, but he wasn't nearly as broad-shouldered. Where Rick's body reminded her of a lineman's, Tom's seemed better built to play basketball. Shannon had always liked football more than basketball.

She shook her head. She was doing it again. Ever since she and Rick had made love that first night, she found herself comparing him to every man she met. Unfortunately for the rest of the male population, Rick set a tough standard.

Oh, Rick!

"I know his parents are dead, but does . . . Rick have any other family we should notify?" she asked, then flushed at Tom's puzzled expression. She supposed that would be a really stupid question coming from a girlfriend, but she wasn't Rick's girlfriend. Right now, she wasn't Rick's anything.

So why did she feel like if he died, most of her soul would die along with him?

"No, Rick doesn't have any family. The last of his family, his grandfather, died several years ago." Tom stood and shoved his hands into his pockets. "I suppose I should call Mary Anne, but I don't think Rick would appreciate the gesture."

"Who's Mary Anne?"

Tom, who'd been staring at his shoes, glanced up sharply. "Are you sure you've been dating my partner?"

Shannon clutched at the pleats in her skirt. "We weren't actually dating," she admitted. "We were just . . . neighbors."

"Lady, he nearly killed himself spitting out your name before he passed out. I don't know what's going on, but he was desperate to see you. So whatever you two didn't have, it was pretty strong."

"We had an affair," she blurted, then colored to the tips of her toes.

One side of Tom's mouth quirked up. "Let me guess. Did this affair happen to end a few days ago?"

It was a good bet her cheeks were the shade of ripe raspberries. "Yes."

He nodded. "That explains why he's been hell to live with

the last few days."

"Me, too," she admitted. "Diane said only a saint wouldn't have wanted to kill me recently."

"So, if you're both so miserable, why are you apart?"

"It's a long story."

"We've got nothing but time, right now."

Shannon opened her mouth, but then a weary-looking man dressed in surgeon's blue came through the door, and Shannon raced over to him. "Is Rick all right? Is he awake? Can we see him, please?"

The doctor looked from her to Tom. "Are you family?"

"Yes!" Shannon blurted.

"Not blood-related," Tom added. "But we're as close as he's got."

The doctor hesitated, then nodded. "It's bad, but it could have been much, much worse."

"He's alive," Shannon breathed, feeling a strong desire to collapse in a heap.

Apparently Tom understood, because he put his arm around her for support. "How bad is it?"

"Your friend sustained a gunshot wound to his right brachial plexus."

"His what?" Tom asked.

"His shoulder," Shannon supplied.

"Oh."

"Right," the doctor said. "The bullet entered his subclavical junction—" Tom opened his mouth, so the doctor pointed to his chest. "Right about here. The bad news is, it's a part of the body that contains many nerves and blood vessels, which explains the massive loss of blood. The good news is, the bullet merely glanced off the clavicle, bruising it." The doctor ran his hand through his damp hair.

"Can you interpret that for me?" Tom asked Shannon.

Shannon tapped Tom's collar bone. "The bullet bruised his collar bone. He'll probably need to keep his arm immobile and in a splint for several weeks."

The doctor nodded, but his look turned grim. "We do have

a bit of a more immediate problem. The loss of blood. Unfortunately for him, he has a very rare type. We don't have any whole blood in that type. We've got the Red Cross working hard to round some up, but until then he's going to have to be tough to stay alive long enough to produce his own, or hang on until we can get some into him."

The image of Rick's blood work report popped into Shannon's head. That's when she remembered she'd been surprised to discover they had the same rare blood type. "AB negative!" she cried.

The doctor and Tom both looked at her like she'd produced a crystal ball. "You don't know that the man's been married before, but you know his blood type?" Tom asked.

Married! Rick had been married? A stab of jealousy sliced through her, but Shannon determinedly ignored it. She waved. "Am I right?"

"Yes," the doctor said.

"That's my type. Take me to your lab to give blood. That's my type."

"Are you serious?"

"Absolutely." She grabbed his wrist desperately. "Take me, I want to give blood."

RICK HAD DIED and somehow conned his way into heaven. He knew that the moment he opened his eyes and saw the angel hovering above him.

Then the pain hit him, and he knew he was more likely in hell. What was Shannon doing in hell?

"Rick?" she whispered.

All he could manage was a grunt. His throat was achingly raw, and his upper body felt like it had been carved up with a machete.

"Rick, it's Shannon."

As if he didn't know. No one else in the world had eyes that big and blue. He nodded slightly, which caused him a great deal of pain. A groan escaped his lips.

He felt her squeeze his left hand, and he tried to squeeze

back. He must have managed it, because she gave him a waterlogged smile.

"The doctor says you're going to be just fine. No major damage."

No major damage? No major damage hurt like all hell.

"You're going to be good as new in a couple of weeks."

"Where . . . " he croaked.

"Fairfax Hospital. You're in good hands."

"Water . . ."

She frowned, and her brows furrowed. "They told me I'm not allowed to give you anything. Let me get a nurse—"

"No!" That word cost him, but he didn't want her to leave him. He clutched her hand harder. "Stay."

"Only for a couple of minutes, the doctor said. But I promise to be back tomorrow."

His eyelids started to feel like lead weights. He fought against unconsciousness. Plenty of time to sleep after she left. In fact, he'd welcome sleep. It would help time pass until she visited him again.

"Shannon," he whispered.

She leaned over him, and he caught a whiff of her scent. A heavenly relief from the antiseptic smell that surrounded him.

"Yes?" she said softly.

He closed his eyes—gathering strength—then opened them again. " . . . missed you."

"Oh, Rick!" she cried. Tears misted her eyes. "I've missed you, too."

"I'm . . . glad."

The squeal of rubber seemed to bounce through his head.

"I'm sorry, Ms. Walsh," a female voice said, "you have to leave now."

Shannon looked up. "He needs water. He's very thirsty."

"Anyone else . . . hurt?"

"No, no one got hurt but . . . you, you idiot."

"Good," he said, feeling an intense need to sleep. But then a thought occurred to him. "Bert."

Shannon gazed down at him, gracing him with an angelic

smile. She stroked his cheek and jaw with soft fingers. The pad of her thumb traced his lips. "Who's Bert?"

"Dog."

Her smile turned into a confused frown. "Dog? What dog?"

"My . . . dog."

"You mean Har—" Her mouth dropped open. "Are you telling me your dog's name is really Bert?"

This was not exactly the setting he'd choose to confess, but he had to make sure someone took care of Bert. "Small . . . joke."

She looked like she'd like to shoot him herself. "Why, you . . . you . . . turkey!"

Rick attempted an innocent smile. He had the feeling it came off looking more like a grimace. "Sorry."

Her mouth was hanging open so far, he could just about see her tonsils. It took her a moment to get the thunderstruck expression off her face.

"Well, we'll discuss that later," she finally said. Squeezing his hand one more time, she gave him a trembly smile. "Far be it from me to kick a man when he's down. Don't you worry. Bert will come stay with me until you get out of here."

"When?"

"Shhhh, go to sleep now. I'll be back tomorrow, I promise."

"Shannon?"

"Yes?"

He opened his mouth, but whatever he'd meant to say drifted away with his consciousness. He closed his mouth, his eyes, and let darkness blanket him.

RICK BEGAN marking the passage of time in terms of Shannon's visits. The first few times he woke and found her there, he felt a little too fuzzy to carry on any sort of intelligent conversation with her.

So she had no idea how much her presence meant to him. Although he realized he was going to survive, the numbness in his shoulder and arm worried him. He usually scratched his way to consciousness with a desperate sense of having lost a limb.

But when he woke up to the sight of Shannon's encouraging, serene smile, the fear that gnawed deep in his belly disappeared.

While he remained conscious, she'd talk about Bert, or the lab, or something outrageous Diane had said. She talked about nothing and everything, with one glaring exception. She never talked about Shannon.

But Rick valued her visits, so he wasn't about to press her to talk about things she considered private. Especially in those first few days, when his mind was so hazy, he might miss something important.

She was there, a bright star in the darkness, and that was all that mattered to Rick. That she was there.

WHEN SHANNON arrived at eleven o'clock one morning of Rick's hospital stay, she panicked when she walked in and found his room empty. She ran out of the room and down to the nurse's station, trying not to scream.

"Where's Rick Hardison? What have you done with him? Where is he?"

The nurse smiled, which immediately stayed her fear. Nurses didn't smile when patients died. Not if they didn't want to quickly follow in the patients' footsteps.

"He's been moved out of ICU."

"Oh, thank God. Where is he?"

"You sure you want to know? He's improved enough to be ornery."

Shannon laughed happily. "I'll take my chances."

The nurse gave Shannon his new room number, and she thanked her, fairly skipping down the steps…the elevator was too slow. As she exited on his new floor and wing, she had to smile. She didn't need anyone directing her to Rick's room. The heated exchange between patient and nurse tipped her off right quick.

" . . . We need to eat to gain our strength!"

"We're going to need a cast on our arm if you don't get that lukewarm chicken broth out of my face!"

Shannon sailed into the room, in time to catch an indignant

"harumph" from the poor nurse, who puffed up like an offended ostrich, then snatched the tray from the table and stomped out of the room on squeaky heels.

Shaking her head, Shannon approached Rick, who was sitting up and looking absolutely delicious in his new found strength.

His skin was bronzed against the snowy white of the gauze covering most of his torso. And his eyes glittered with lucidity and irritation. But when he spotted her the irritation vanished. "Hi, angel."

"Hi. What are you up to, besides harassing the poor nursing staff?"

"Come here and I'll show you."

His sensual gaze pulled at her, had her leaning toward him, and before she knew it, they were kissing hungrily. Rick's hand slid around her neck to her nape. He held her against his lips, refusing to break the kiss too soon.

Shannon finally pulled back, breathless. "You're definitely on the road to recovery."

"In part, thanks to you."

Her eyes went wide. "Me?"

"The doctor mentioned this morning that you gave blood for me."

His eyes glistened, and Shannon felt her cheeks heat up. "It was the least I could do."

"Well, the least you could do just might have saved me." He grinned. "I have feeling in my arm today."

"Oh, Rick, that's wonderful!" Without thinking, she brushed a stray strand of his hair from his cheek. "I knew you'd make a full recovery."

He trapped her hand against his face. While he gazed into her eyes, he turned his head slightly, then placed a soft, seductive kiss in the center of her palm.

Shannon's body caught fire, and she sucked in a breath. In truth, being deprived of Rick's lovemaking for the last ten days had wound her up like a tight spring. With just a light touch of his lips on her skin, he released the coil and her insides rattled from the desire that shot through her.

This was not good. In the last several days, she'd been telling herself that her fear for Rick was just the common garden variety—one human being caring about the welfare of another.

But her reaction to his touch, his kiss, was not the common garden variety of a woman responding to an attractive man. It was Rick, and only Rick. His lips, and only his lips. His hands, and only his hands. She responded to the man, not the species. And it scared the devil out of her that she might never respond to another man this way. That Rick had ruined her for her future husband.

She snatched her hand back, and scratched her palm where it tingled. Glancing around the room, she noted all the flowers. He apparently had plenty of friends. "Police health insurance must be very generous for you to get a private room."

His eyes turned guarded, and he just shrugged. "I like my privacy."

"I brought you some books and magazines," she said, waving at the pile she'd dropped on his bed stand.

"Thank you."

"I hope you like mysteries."

He kept silent for a moment as he searched her face. "As long as I can eventually solve them."

Flustered by the meaningful look he shot her, she thrust a card at him. "This is from Bert, who misses you terribly."

He took it with his good hand. Dropping it in his lap, he tried to open it, but couldn't quite manage. Shannon could see the frustration in the stern set of his features.

She grabbed the card. "Here, let me help."

"I can do it!" he said, his lower lip almost pouting.

Shannon stifled a smile. "Listen, Mr. Macho, get used to the fact that you're going to need help for a couple of weeks. It's nothing to be ashamed of."

"I'll manage."

"No, you won't," she said, handing him the card and tossing the envelope in the trash. "When you get out of here, you're coming to live with me until you can use your arm again."

Rick was reading the front of the card "from Bert" so it took a moment for her words to sink in. When they did, he went still, then slowly raised his gaze to hers.

By the stunned look on her face, he knew that she hadn't considered that offer before making it. His first reaction was to say, "Thanks, but no thanks." Rick had been taking care of himself his entire life. He hadn't needed anyone when he was a boy, and he didn't need anyone now.

Still, he debated. What would it be like living with Shannon, letting her take care of him? Would she open up, share herself with him? Maybe that was just what the doctor ordered, so to speak. Maybe she'd get on his nerves, and his attraction to her would collapse under the weight of Shannon's annoying personality.

She certainly wouldn't be able to distract him with sex, more's the pity. At least not for several days. In that time she'd have no choice but to talk to him. Maybe even, perish the thought, share personal information with him.

Shannon looked like she was holding her breath, waiting for his answer. Hoping he'd say no.

"Thanks," he said, before she fainted from oxygen deprivation. "That's really nice of you. I'd really appreciate that."

Her breath left her in a noisy whoosh. "Unless . . . unless you'd rather . . . sleep in your own bed. I could . . . just come down and see to things, help you out . . ."

He returned his attention to Bert's card, before he burst out laughing and jarred his shoulder. There was one thing he already knew about Shannon. She could never win at poker. "No, I think your place would be much more comfortable. I have the feeling climbing steps is going to be painful for a few days." He chuckled at the card. Shannon had signed it, "Love, Bert," then had drawn a paw print beneath it.

He glanced up. "Unless, you're withdrawing the offer."

"Oh, no, of course not. It's just, well, I didn't know if you'd prefer to be surrounded by your own things."

"I'd prefer to be surrounded by you."

The woman he'd been having an affair with for a

month—who'd let him learn her body's secrets in every imaginable way, who'd turned to him countless times deep in the night, silently demanding her pleasure—blushed.

She was an anomaly. She gave everything to him in bed, and nothing out of it. He liked the former about her, and was really beginning to hate the latter.

But if he stayed under her roof, basically living with her, letting her take tender-loving care of him, how could she possibly hold back? How could she remain aloof? With any luck, she couldn't. With any luck, and a little planning on his part, by the time he returned to his own home, he was going to know everything he wanted to know about Shannon Walsh.

He laughed softly at the thought. For the first time in his life, he was going to plot the seduction, not of a woman's body, but of her mind.

"What's so funny?" Shannon asked suspiciously.

"Nothing. I'm just glad to have company."

"Can you handle more?" Fletch asked from the doorway.

"Good company, yes," Rick retorted. "Which definitely leaves you out."

Ignoring him, Fletch shot Shannon one of his charm-boy smiles, and strolled into the room. He went straight to her, and kissed her on the cheek. This did not make Rick happy. In fact, this made Rick furious. What the hell had happened while he'd been fighting for his life?

"Hi, sweetheart," Fletch said. "Is he unbearable today?"

Shannon smiled up at Fletch, accepting his arm looped over her shoulder quite easily. "Unbearable. You should have seen the violence he unleashed on a bowl of chicken broth."

"Hey folks," Rick said irritably. "Nothing happened to his hearing. And Fletch, get your dirty hands off m—her."

Holy hell! Had he almost said, "My woman?" He scowled at both of them. They looked like Barbie and Ken, standing side-by-side. The perfect couple. He'd bet Shannon's parents would pant with happiness if she brought Fletch home to meet mom and dad.

Fletch's slow smile, and his even slower removal of his arm

from her person told Rick he knew exactly what Rick had almost said. Lucky for Fletch, Rick wasn't armed at the moment.

Shannon cleared her throat. "Well, I think I'll go get a soda and give you two a chance to talk."

"You don't have to go," Rick said, a strange feeling of emptiness landing in the pit of his stomach at the thought of her gone. "There's nothing we—"

"Thanks, Shannon," Fletch interrupted. "Would you get me a Dr. Pepper?"

"Sure." Shannon escaped before Fletch could even reach for his wallet.

Rick glared at Fletch. "What the hell was that all about? And what the hell are you doing kissing her like that? And if you touch her again, I swear I'm going to—"

Fletch burst out laughing and held up both hands. "Whoa, buddy! Relax. Sharing a few days of fear for a mutual friend has a way of bringing people close."

"How close?" Rick growled, scowling at Fletch's prep-boy clothes. He'd never had a problem with Fletch's wardrobe before, but today it was really getting on his nerves. Now that he thought about it, he didn't think he'd ever seen a wrinkle in the man's always perfectly creased pants. That was unnatural.

Fletch leaned indolently on the table beside Rick's bed. "Close enough to realize the woman's crazy about you."

Rick pointed at Fletch's nose. "And don't you forget it." His frown disappeared. "How do you know that?"

Fletch shrugged a shoulder. "Maybe the fact that she was almost hysterical with fear for your sorry hide."

"She's just a bleeding heart," Rick argued, although the thought that she might care just a little warmed his insides. When Fletch didn't continue to offer proof, he added, "She'd worry about an injured snake."

"That's right. She did. A few days ago."

"Screw you." He gingerly scratched his injured shoulder. "She's taken, so back off."

"I thought it was over between you two."

"Well, you thought wrong. In fact, she asked me to stay

with her so she can take care of me while I recuperate."

"Take . . . " Fletch sputtered. "Take care . . . of you!" He burst out laughing. "If there was ever a man in the world who didn't need a nursemaid, it's you."

"You mention that in front of her, and I'll . . . start a rumor you like to wear pantyhose."

"That's low."

"I'm desperate."

Fletch's grin disappeared. "You really are, aren't you?"

Rick flexed his good shoulder. "Not permanently. I just didn't get a chance to get bored with the relationship."

"Right." His eyes strayed to Rick's bandaged shoulder, and his expression turned grim. "You scared the hell out of me, buddy."

"Sorry."

"That was a stupid thing to do, you know."

"I know."

"You're lucky you didn't buy it."

"I know."

They looked at each other. Rick recognized the naked fear in Fletch's eyes. They'd been partners for five years and had clicked from the first day. Fletch was the closest thing Rick had to a brother, and Rick knew seeing him get shot had scared the hell out of his partner. He held out his left hand.

Fletch blinked, then took it.

"Thanks, man," Rick said.

Swallowing, Fletch said, "Don't make me go through that again."

"I'll do my best." His hand dropped back to his lap. "And thanks for tracking down Shannon."

"No problem."

"Now tell me, what's the name of the little slug who shot me?"

"David John Keggler. Career criminal at the ripe old age of sixteen. D.A.'s office is planning to try him as an adult. Attempted murder."

"A Crow, right?"

"A Crow. He's being called a hero by his gang buddies."

"Of course he is. Shooting a cop is a badge of honor."

They were silent for a moment as both thought of the mindset of a group of kids who took murder so lightly.

Finally Fletch said, "You up to more company?"

"Who?" Rick asked, annoyed because the only company he wanted was Shannon's.

"Kid named Tony. Says he's your friend."

"Tony's here?"

"Sitting down the hall. He's been here every day. Seems like a nice kid."

"Of course I want to see him," Rick said. "Let him see the result of gang violence."

"Rick, he was scared to death for you. I think the lesson's been learned. Don't be hard on him."

Laying his head back on his pillow, he stared up at the ceiling. "I know." His gaze swung back to Fletch. "I'll be good. Send him in."

"Something you should know first."

"What?"

"David Keggler claimed that you drew your weapon first."

"What!" Rick exploded, then winced when his shoulder screamed in protest. "That's utter bull. I hope you laughed in the kid's face."

Fletch frowned. "Actually, I couldn't guarantee that you hadn't."

Rick stared at Fletch like he'd sprouted green antennas.

Fletch shrugged. "I told them you wouldn't do that, but I couldn't say you didn't. Your back was to me. I couldn't see what you were doing, and you were blocking Keggler, so I couldn't see what he was doing either. Damn, Rick, if I'd have seen him pull the piece—"

"Hey, don't start trying to take any credit here, pal. You couldn't have known." He blew out his breath. "Let me guess. I.A.D.'s going to investigate."

"Nope. Your gun was in your holster. That was good enough for them."

Rick nodded, relieved. Like any intelligent, self-respecting cop, he possessed a healthy distrust of Internal Affairs. "Send in the kid, partner."

Fletch stared at him a moment. "My, my, we seem to have developed a fondness for several people lately."

Rick graced Fletch with a disgusted look. "I'm just making sure the idiot kid stays alive long enough to have a future."

"Sure you are."

Hating that Fletch thought him sentimental, he glared. "Bring him in."

AFTER DAWDLING over her soda as long as she could, Shannon reluctantly headed back to Rick's room. Her aversion to returning had nothing to do with Rick, and everything to do with her.

Why had she invited him to stay at her house? The last thing she needed was to have him around constantly, reminding her just how very attracted she was to him. The last thing she needed was to get accustomed to having him in every part of her life. The last thing she needed was to play house with him.

Because she had a sinking feeling playing house would feel too real.

Shannon had goals. She had responsibilities, to herself and her parents. Rick didn't figure into the equation. He just didn't.

Unfortunately, the thought of anyone else completing the equation sent a shudder rippling through her. Rick was all wrong for her. So why did he feel so right?

Shannon stopped just outside his open door, resting her forehead on the cool wall. Somehow she had to get Rick Hardison out of her system. Somehow she had to get him out of her life. Somehow she had to be happy about that.

Rick's voice drifted out to her, and she smiled slightly, enjoying his rumbling baritone. " . . . catch you with any of those young thugs, I'm gonna kick your ass."

"You won't," a higher-pitched male voice responded. "That scene is for losers."

"You got that right." There was a short silence, then Rick

continued. "How's your game coming along?"

"I'll kick *your* ass when you get better."

"Dream on."

"I'm gettin' good. You'll see." The younger man paused. "I've been hanging at the Y. Met a couple of guys there that are going out for the team, like me. We've been kinda practicing together."

"Nice guys?"

"They're chilly, I guess." Another pause. "You gonna be able to toss a ball around soon?"

"Give me a couple of weeks. I'll be able to stomp all over you again."

Tony snorted. "Yeah, right."

Shannon rolled her eyes. The blustery male testosterone was practically rolling out of Rick's hospital room in a fog.

Suddenly realizing she was, in essence, eavesdropping again, she straightened from the wall and rounded the corner, into the room. Rick grinned at her, which caused Tony to turn. Just like the last time, he blushed deep crimson when he spotted her.

Shannon had no idea why she unnerved the boy so much. She tried to smile kindly, but he'd already dropped his gaze to the baseball cap crushed in his hands. "Well, guess I gotta go," he mumbled. He put the cap on backward.

Rick's good hand shot out and grabbed Tony's arm. "Wait." He turned his dark gaze on Shannon. "Would you mind if I invite Tony to come visit me some days at your house? While you're at work, I could probably use the company."

"Not at all," Shannon replied, the disturbing image of Rick ensconced in her home making her voice sound a little breathless.

Tony's jaw dropped. "You're scrappin' with her?"

Rick frowned. "Watch your language in front of the lady."

The lady had no idea what the boy had just said. Somehow she didn't think she wanted to know.

Releasing Tony's arm, Rick asked. "Will you stop by occasionally?"

"Yeah, if you want," Tony said with a casual shrug.

Shannon wasn't fooled. The kid was thrilled that Rick asked.

Rick slapped his arm. "Good. Starting tomorrow, you'll find me at Shannon's."

It was Shannon's turn to gape at him. "Tomorrow?" she squeaked.

A slow smile spread over Rick's face. "Tomorrow," he repeated, making it sound more like a promise than a time frame.

# Chapter Seven

SHANNON STUFFED another pillow behind Rick's back. Satisfied he was comfortable lying on her couch, she pulled the TV remote, a book and a huge plastic mug of soda within his grasp on the coffee table.

She straightened. "There. Think you'll survive until I get home tonight?"

"I'll be fine."

She fussed with her blouse collar, reluctant to leave him. Strangely, as Fletch had helped her get Rick settled in her house, she'd felt none of the dread she'd expected to feel as she placed his toothbrush beside hers, and put his clothes away in the spare bedroom.

Instead, she felt a bubbling anticipation. Having his masculine presence in her house constantly would be . . . thrilling. Exciting.

Temporary.

That thought reassured her. It was all temporary. She could enjoy Rick's company for a couple of weeks, maybe even find herself getting tired of him. Then he'd move out, and she'd move on. She'd have her delicious memories to carry with her for the rest of her life. Her proper life. Her upstanding, proper life. Her *boring*, upstanding, proper life.

She frowned. She had to stop using that word. It only depressed her. Just because she was going to fulfill her parents' dream of marrying a good, pious man didn't necessarily mean he'd bore her. He might not excite her like Rick did, but that was a good thing. She'd shorten her life span considerably if she married a man who affected her like Rick affected her. Her heart would probably wear out before she turned fifty.

"What's the matter, angel?" Rick asked her. "You having second thoughts?"

Shannon shook her head, biting down on her lower lip. "No. I'm glad you're here."

His eyebrows shot up. "You are?"

She nodded, then grinned impishly. "I like having you helpless and in my care."

One side of his mouth lifted, revealing a slight dimple in his cheek she'd never noticed before. "Should I be shaking in my sling?"

She leaned over him, the devil in her rearing up. "Only if you don't obey my every command."

His good hand came up to caress her neck, his thumb tracing her jaw. "I'll be a good boy, I promise."

"I don't want you to be a good boy," she murmured, her eyes fluttering closed as she gave into the pressure of his hand to lower her lips to his.

Rick kissed her, just a light, feather stroke of his lips against hers. Shannon sighed, savoring his tenderness. She knew he'd turn that tender touch into a ravishing assault that made her senses reel, with just a sign from her.

Unfortunately, he was in no condition to assault her senses. Besides, she needed to get back to work. Reluctantly, she broke the kiss, but only raised her head an inch or so. She opened her eyes and drank in his harsh features. "You're a beautiful man, Rick," she whispered.

His knuckles froze on her cheek. "You think so?"

"Oh, yes."

"Long hair and all?"

"Long hair and all."

"Shannon?"

"Yes?"

"Do you realize your blood is coursing in my veins?"

"Yes," she whispered.

"That makes you a part of me."

Shannon was so mesmerized by the smoldering look in his obsidian eyes, by the sexy rumble of his voice, that it took her a moment to assimilate his words. When she did, she straightened abruptly.

The sentiment disturbed her more than she could say. It seemed to imply a permanence that she knew wasn't possible. Avoiding his eyes, she stepped around the coffee table and snatched up her purse.

"Well, don't forget to take your medication," she said in a bright voice that wouldn't fool an idiot. "And the aspirin's right there if you need it. I'll be home around six."

Then she hightailed it out of there before Rick could respond.

Rick shifted on the couch, then spat a string of curses as jagged shards of pain stabbed across his shoulder and down his arm. Why had he been so excited about getting feeling back? he wondered. Now that he realized what kind of feeling would return, he wished his shoulder and arm had stayed blessedly numb until they'd healed entirely.

His discomfort wasn't the only thing souring his mood. The memory of Shannon's face when he'd made that ridiculous statement also formed knots in his belly.

What the hell had he been thinking? Wherever had that thought come from, and why in hell had he been stupid enough to voice it?

And why did Shannon appear so scared by it? Every drop of blood had drained from her face, and her eyes had gone big as swimming pools. He might as well have told her he would be murdering her in her sleep that night.

Rick had never given a damn what people thought of him. So why had Shannon's calling him beautiful meant so much to him? Meant enough that he came up with that disgustingly corny observation?

He cursed again, and started flicking through channels, not taking in anything on the TV. Would a simple haircut and the removal of an earring change her mind about him?

He didn't think so. Shannon somehow sensed his background without ever having asked. And her instincts on that were right on. Her dark side felt drawn to him, but he wasn't good enough for the long haul.

Jabbing at the remote button irritably, Rick turned off the television. The hell with Shannon Walsh. He didn't need her kind in his life. He'd already been taken in by one female who wanted him to be something he wasn't. He hadn't changed for Mary Anne, and he certainly wasn't going to change for Shannon.

RICK MUST BE in a lot of pain, Shannon thought, glancing out of the kitchen into the living room. He'd barely said two words to her since she'd arrived home fifteen minutes ago, and both of them had been clipped and vibrating with annoyance.

She shrugged, trying not to take it personally. The doctor had warned her he'd be a royal pain for a few days, due to the injury, and probably worse after that, because of his immobility. She'd just have to ignore him.

"I hope you like chicken and dumplings," she called out, while she poured chopped onions into the Dutch oven mixture of water, chicken breasts, carrots and celery.

He muttered something, but she couldn't understand what it was. She dropped a bay leaf into the broth, then walked out to the living room. "What?"

"I said I don't even know what the hell chicken and dumplings are," he growled, studiously ignoring her and staring intently at a Rocky and Bullwinkle cartoon on the TV.

"Oh, you've been deprived," she said cheerfully. "It's a good old-fashioned Pennsylvania Dutch meal."

"Well, no wonder I've never heard of it," he said, his voice caked with sarcasm. "My mother's specialty was TV dinners."

Shannon's smile collapsed. Her heart went out to the little boy who'd never had a normal childhood. She hadn't exactly had a normal childhood either, considering the daughter of the town preacher always had to put up a solid, righteous front for the congregation. But at least she'd had a mother who'd cooked supper every night, who'd made certain Shannon had warm clothes and clean bed sheets. "I'm sorry, Rick," she said softly.

If anything, his scowl deepened. "Sorry for what? For my misspent youth?" He laughed. Or it was a poor imitation of a laugh. "What do you care?"

"Of course, I care!" she snapped.

"Like hell!" he snapped back. "I could have been born on Mars and you wouldn't know it. You don't know a damn thing about me!"

"I know you're a sulky little baby when you're in pain!" she retorted, then stuck her nose in the air, spun on her heel and marched back to the kitchen.

She heard the curses he muttered, but she ignored them. She knew a lot more about Rick Hardison than he realized. And she ached for him, admired him for overcoming the bad breaks he'd been handed.

But she didn't need or deserve this abuse, she thought irritably, as she swiped at the skins of the potatoes. Let him sulk.

"Is there any liquor in this house?" Rick boomed, making Shannon jump.

"Yes, but you're not getting any!" she shouted back.

"Why not?"

She tossed down the potato peeler and walked to the doorway. "Because you're on medication, you big baby, and you're not supposed to mix the two."

He scowled at her. "The medication is only pain-killers, and they're not working."

Wiping her hands down her apron, she said, "Take an extra aspirin."

"I want a beer!"

"Tough, I don't have any beer."

"What do you have?"

"Wine."

He muttered a curse. "Fine. I'll take a glass."

She opened her mouth, about to refuse him. Then she shut it again with a click of her teeth. Whirling, she went to the refrigerator and grabbed the wine. Pouring it, she tossed out a couple of her own swear words. They weren't as colorful as his, but they made her feel a whole lot better.

She took the wine out to him and dumped it on the table. "Anything else, your Lordship?"

He bared his white teeth in a feral smile. "I'll let you know."

Shannon bobbed a curtsy. "Yes, master."

His hand snaked out and wrapped around her wrist. "Sarcasm doesn't become you, angel."

"Sulking doesn't become you, brat."

"I am not sulking!"

Shannon merely snorted, then snatched back her wrist. "I've known two-year-olds more mature than you."

"In case you didn't notice, I got shot recently."

"I'm beginning to empathize with the gunman."

If it was possible for a grown man to pout, Rick was pouting. Shannon almost laughed aloud. God, the man was impossible.

"Florence Nightingale, you're not," he muttered.

"Oh, yeah, and you're the perfect patient."

She patted Bert's head when he nudged her hand. "Your dad's a royal pain, isn't he, sweetie?"

Bert barked his agreement.

"Traitor," Rick muttered.

Bert ignored him, trotting happily beside Shannon as she returned to the kitchen.


"THIRDS?" Shannon asked Rick, as he wiped his second helping of chicken and dumplings clean.

"Yes, please," he said, handing his plate over to her. He tried to ignore the humorous gleam in her eye as she rose and went to refill it.

The delicious meal had done wonders for his disposition. One more tiny piece of the Shannon Walsh puzzle fell into place. She knew how to cook.

He liked that in a woman, because he sure as hell loved to eat.

Shannon set a heaping plate of food in front of him, then sat down again to pick at her own. No wonder the woman stayed so slender. She barely ate enough to keep a gnat alive.

He quickly cleaned his plate again, savoring the tastes. Taking a final bite of mashed potatoes doused in chicken gravy, he closed his eyes and moaned his appreciation. After he swallowed, he set down his fork and wiped his lips with a napkin. "That was heaven."

She smiled, obviously pleased with the compliment. While he sat temporarily in her good graces, he slipped in a question. "Are you from Pennsylvania?"

Her smile dissolved. "How'd you know that?"

Rick shrugged his good shoulder, feigning an air of mild interest. "You said this was a Pennsylvania Dutch meal."

"Oh, that's right, I did." Suddenly she was vitally interested in her dinner.

Rick took her wrist, stopping her from sawing the poor chicken into shreds. "Look at me."

Slowly, she raised her gaze.

"Shannon, this isn't going to work."

"What do you mean?"

"Since sex is out of the question for the next few days, it's going to get awfully boring around here if we can't talk about anything personal. I mean, I guess we could discuss sex, but that could get very uncomfortable, very quickly."

She opened her mouth, but he kept right on talking. "Since it's supposedly unwise to discuss religion or politics, and since neither of us has kids to brag about, that doesn't leave much, does it?"

"Not much," she admitted.

"I'm not trying to invade your privacy, Shannon. I'm not asking you to reveal your deep, dark secrets. Call me funny, but I just happen to be curious about the woman I'm sleeping with."

She stared at him for a moment. "You already know my darkest secret."

"I do?"

Nodding vigorously, she said, "Oh, yes."

"And what secret's that?"

"You know . . . you know about my fantasy."

Rick had no idea what the hell she was talking about. "I do?"

"Yes."

"What fantasy is that?"

She gaped at him a little. "You, of course."

"Me?"

"Yes, you. You're my fantasy."

Any other time, Rick might have been flattered. But he didn't want to be Shannon's fantasy. He wanted to be her reality. "I'm not a fantasy, Shannon."

"Could have fooled me."

"I'm a man. Flesh and blood."

"A fantasy man."

"No, dammit!" he said, hitting the coffee table with his fist.

Shannon jumped and nearly dumped her plate.

"A fantasy implies something unreal. I assure you, I'm very real." He touched his bandage. "I bleed, I have feelings. And I don't particularly like being used."

"Used?" she repeated blankly.

"That's right. Used."

"Who's using you?"

It was Rick's turn to gape. Was she serious? She sure looked it. "Well I can name one person, for starters."

"Who?"

"You."

She took the gaping right back from him. "Me?"

"That's right," he said, his indignation growing. "You."

"How am I using you?"

Rick grabbed back the gape. "You can't be serious."

"I have no idea what you're talking about."

"Are you going to deny you use me for sex?"

Her jaw dropped even further. "I . . . thought that was mutual."

"Well, maybe at first."

Shannon stood, taking her plate with her. "I . . . think I'll just clean up. Are you finished?"

"Yes."

While he waited for Shannon to return, he drummed his fingers against his thigh. And drummed. And drummed. Either chicken and dumplings took a hundred pots to prepare, or Shannon was taking her good old time cleaning up.

About a century later she returned to the living room and kept herself busy straightening things that didn't need to be straightened.

Rick finally had enough. "Shannon!"

She nearly hit the ceiling. "What?"

"Come here."

She didn't look too thrilled, but she returned to her seat.

"Are you going to answer me?"

"Answer you about what?"

"About using me."

She held up her hands and laughed helplessly. "Like I said, I thought it was mutual."

"Well, it was. But now, well, now I'd like us to be friends, too."

"Why?" Shannon asked suspiciously. She couldn't believe she was sitting facing every woman's fantasy man, and he was complaining about being used. Somehow, she felt this was a historic event, but she didn't know why.

He shot her a brooding look. "Because there's more to life than sex."

Definitely a historic event. The thought of getting to know Rick seemed almost more intimate than sleeping with him. But really it wasn't such a frightening prospect. After all, she'd be gone in three months, and after some time and distance, she'd forget all about her fantasy man. "How do you propose we move from lovers to friends?"

The smile that lit his face dazzled her. How he could transform from a devilishly handsome stud to a boyishly adorable teddy bear was a mystery.

A mystery. Yesterday, he'd implied she was a mystery. And in a flash of insight, she realized he was a mystery to her as well. And she wanted to solve the mystery of Rick Hardison.

"Well," he said, rubbing his chin, "I know we're doing this a little backwards, but if I remember correctly, people become friends by getting to know each other and finding qualities in common, or that complement each other."

Shannon laughed. "I don't think you and I have a thing in common."

"Oh, I don't know about that," he answered, winking suggestively.

"Besides that," Shannon amended.

"Well, let's find out. I'll tell you what. You ask me a question, then I'll ask you. Eventually we'll find something in common."

"Okay."

"So ask."

"What happened to your marriage?"

Obviously, he hadn't been expecting that one. He nearly choked on the wine he'd been sipping. "Who told you about my marriage?"

"Fletch."

"That big-mouthed, pretty boy. When I get my hands on him—"

"He didn't mean to!"

"Oh, really? How does one go about accidentally letting something like that slip?"

"He was just amazed that I knew your blood type, but didn't know you had an ex-wife."

"Oh," he said, scratching at his bandage.

"Stop scratching," Shannon ordered. "So, are you going to tell me, or have you changed your mind about sharing?"

Very carefully, he set down his wine goblet. "What do you want to know?"

"How long were you married?"

"Less than a year."

For some reason, that didn't surprise Shannon. What surprised her was that he'd ever gotten married in the first place. He just didn't seem like a marrying type of guy. "How long ago was that?"

"Two years ago."

"That reminds me. How old are you, anyway?"

"Thirty-four."

"So, what happened to the marriage?"

"Let's just say, we had incompatible goals."

"Meaning what?"

"Meaning she didn't approve of my life choices."

"Such as?"

"Such as staying on the force."

"What did she want you to do instead?"

He opened his mouth, stopped, then closed it slowly. After a moment, he shrugged. "Something more . . . prestigious."

"She had to know what you did for a living before she married you."

"She thought she could re-channel my energies."

Shannon smiled. "Was she really that stupid?"

Rick grinned back at her. She decided he had the sexiest smile she'd ever seen. "Apparently."

"Anyone can take one look at you and know you're very strong-willed."

"Is that a nice way of saying I'm stubborn?"

"Determined." Shannon laughed. "You told me so yourself."

"So I did. My turn."

She found herself filling with anticipation. Why, she couldn't fathom. "Go ahead."

"How is it that you've made it this far—what are you, twenty-seven, twenty-eight?—without some guy snatching you up?"

"I'm thirty-one." Pushing back her mop of hair, she said, "I don't know. It's not like I don't want to get married. I do. I just . . . have never met anyone who filled the order."

"Filled the order?" he asked, cocking his head.

Shannon brought her knees up to her chest and wrapped her arms around them. "I guess that sounds stupid. As long as I can remember, I've had this image of what my husband should be like."

"And what's that?" he asked, his eyes suddenly hooded.

Shannon waved. "Some of the usual things, I guess. Tall, handsome, successful—"

"You mean, rich," he interrupted, and he didn't sound pleased.

Shannon took exception to his tone. Her chin hiked up. "Not necessarily. Success doesn't always translate into dollars. I'd just want him to love what he does for a living, and be good at it."

There was just the hint of disbelief glittering in his eyes. "Go on, what else are you looking for?"

Resting her chin on one knee, she continued. "He should be a solid, upstanding member of the community. His reputation should be beyond reproach. He'll have strong moral values. He'll—What?" she asked, as she saw him snort.

"Last I heard, the Pope wasn't looking to get married."

"I'm not—" Her feet dropped to the floor. "That is what it sounds like I'm looking for, isn't it?"

"Do men like that really exist?"

"Of course." She sighed. "In fact, Mark meets all the requirements."

"Who's Mark?"

"My boyfriend."

In one swift move, Rick swung his feet to the floor and stood, only wincing slightly. "Your what?"

Shannon stood up, too. "Rick, lie down."

Bert, who'd been snoozing in the corner, dutifully dragged himself up to a sitting position. Shannon looked at him. "Come!" Gratefully, Bert plopped back down.

"Let me get this straight," Rick growled. "You've got a boyfriend."

"Well, I did."

"It's over?"

"Not exactly."

"What is it, exactly?"

"I . . . I'm not sure."

"Does this Mark jerk know about me?"

"Of course not!"

Apparently, that was the wrong answer. Anger shimmered from his body in waves. "You didn't feel it necessary," he said, his voice gravelly, "to inform me that you were involved with another man?"

Shannon gulped. How'd they get into this, anyway? "I . . . didn't think it made a difference to you and me."

His eyebrow quirked up dangerously. "Oh, really?" He moved around the table, bearing down on her. Even injured he had a male grace she found extremely exciting. Only the thunderous look on his face kept her from smiling appreciatively. "Why is that, Shannon? What is it about me that leads you to believe I'd willingly play the 'other man?'"

"But you're not! Not really. Mark and I have an agreement. As long as I'm in DC, I'm free to . . . see other men."

He glared down at her. "What do you mean, as long as you're in DC?"

"Maybe you better sit."

Even in his sleep, Bert lifted his paw.

"I'll stand, thank you."

This getting to know each other thing wasn't going real well. Considering Rick looked like he wanted to strangle her at the moment, she decided it was actually a disaster. What else could go wrong?

As if on cue, the phone rang.

Shannon ignored it. She had the sinking feeling that with the way her luck was going right now, the call had to be from Mark.

After the third ring, Rick smiled dangerously. "Aren't you going to answer that?"

"I . . . wasn't planning on it."

"Want me to answer it for you?"

Shannon scrambled to the phone, praying it was an AT&T salesman.

It wasn't an AT&T salesman and it wasn't Mark. It was Fletch. Breathing her relief, Shannon greeted him enthusiastically.

"Well, now, sweetheart, you sound awfully cheerful for a

woman who has to put up with a grumpy patient."

Shannon laughed, eyeing a scowling Rick. "You have no idea how grumpy."

"Can I talk to the chump?"

"By all means."

Shannon handed the phone to Rick, then skipped out of the room, grateful for the respite. She needed time to pull herself together.

She dropped into the chair at her vanity and brushed her hair absently. Why did Rick seem so bent out of shape? She wasn't exactly on intimate terms with the rules for having love affairs, but she was pretty certain there weren't supposed to be any strings. And suddenly Rick was acting awfully stringy.

What did he care if she had a boyfriend back home? Why, if the situation were reversed . . .

An unexpected stab of jealousy pierced her. What would she do if Rick had a girlfriend? She certainly wouldn't sleep with him. And if she found out about the woman after the fact, she'd feel awfully used.

Testing her emotions, she thought about Mark. How would she feel if he started dating other women? Another stab knifed through her, but not the same kind. If she were to be honest, it felt more like relief than jealousy.

What did that say? Plenty. It said plenty. She wasn't in love with Mark, and she wasn't going to marry him. Not in three months, not ever. She couldn't possibly marry a man who inspired absolutely no jealousy on her part.

Was it so wrong to want to be madly in love with her husband? And why couldn't she find a man who made her feel like Rick made her feel? She wanted a husband who made her weak-kneed with love. Rick made her weak-kneed all right, but it had nothing to do with love. *Face it, Shannon, you're a sinful, lustful creature.*

She'd wanted to get the wanderlust out of her system before settling down and starting a family, but by getting involved with Rick, her plan had backfired. Because she now knew without a doubt that a basic requirement necessary to her happiness was an all-consuming passion for her husband.

Passion like the one she felt for the man . . . reflected in her mirror.

Shannon whirled toward the door, her heart thudding with that passion she'd just been contemplating. "Oh, I must have been daydreaming. I didn't hear you knock."

"I didn't knock."

Her eyes narrowed. "Now see here, buster—"

"No, you see here, sweetheart," he said, strolling into the room. "I'm sick of the games you're playing."

Her mouth dropped open. "Games?"

"Games. You're toying with me, and I don't like it one bit."

He reached her. His eyes were glittering pools of anger and frustration. Grasping her shoulder, he pulled her close. Then his lips were on hers, hot and demanding.

Shannon vaguely considered resisting his kiss, but it would have been too much trouble, and besides she loved the way he kissed her.

Rick had this unique ability to arouse Shannon with his lips alone. She felt his kisses all the way down to the very center of her lusty soul. This kiss was no different. By the time he finished ravishing her mouth, Shannon felt as if he'd touched every inch of her.

She gazed up at him, his usually sharp features a little fuzzy at the moment. But his eyes weren't fuzzy. They were dark and gleaming with so many emotions, she couldn't name them all. But she recognized one clearly.

He wanted to make love.

She placed a shaking hand on the left side of his chest, careful to avoid the bandage. "Rick, we can't. You'll hurt your shoulder."

"Not if you handle me carefully."

She drew in a breath, searching for sanity. "I'm afraid I'll hurt you."

"You didn't seem to worry about that when you got involved with me."

Shannon blinked. Somehow she felt she'd missed a step in

logic here. "Huh?" was the most intelligent thing she could think of to say.

"When were you planning to tell me you have a boyfriend?"

"I wasn't."

"When were you planning on telling me your stay in DC is temporary?"

"I wasn't."

"Dammit, Shannon! Didn't you think I had a right to know?"

"No. I didn't think it was necessary with an affair."

A muscle started working in his jaw. His hand dropped from her neck. "And what if I had been stupid enough to fall in love with you? What would you have done then?"

She waved that ludicrous scenario away. "You wouldn't have. You're not a fall-in-love type of guy."

The muscle in his jaw fairly jumped through his skin. "You have no idea what type of guy I am, Shannon. You've never bothered to find out."

"I thought that was for the best," she whispered.

He glared at her. "All I am to you is a body. Well forget it, angel. You're done using me. Find your jollies elsewhere."

He turned on his heel and stalked out of the bedroom.

As she stared after him, gape-mouthed, Shannon told herself she shouldn't feel so bereft. After all, it would end, one way or another, soon enough.

She was just very, very unhappy that it was ending this way. He'd almost looked hurt. But that was ridiculous.

She followed him out to the living room, fully expecting to find him gathering his belongings. Instead, she found him watching Bugs Bunny.

"You're not leaving?"

He looked at her blandly. "Hell, no. I figure the stud service I've performed the last month more than earns my keep for the next few days."

Her joy overshadowed her irritation. Which was a strange thing in and of itself. She should kick the cocky bastard out on his rump. His nice rump. His very, very nice rump.

Instead, she was looking forward to the next several days like she had looked forward to nothing else in her life. Because whether Rick Hardison admitted it or not, he still wanted her. She could work with that.

She looked forward to it.

# Chapter Eight

"BATH TIME!" Shannon announced two nights later after supper.

Rick glanced up from the book he was reading, the surprise on his face comical. Then his eyes narrowed as he took in her innocent smile. "I washed up this morning."

She waggled the sponge in her hand. "Men are notoriously rotten at cleaning themselves."

"If you think I'm going to let you give me a bath, you are sadly mistaken."

Shannon managed a hurt frown. "Are you afraid of me?"

"Damn straight."

"Little old me?"

"Little old you."

"What are you afraid I'll do?"

"Touch me."

Undaunted, Shannon sauntered over to him, putting a little extra swing in her hips, the way she'd practiced in the kitchen while she'd prepared supper. She supposed she must be doing something right when she saw his Adam's apple bob up and down a couple of times.

She scraped a fingernail lightly down his beard-darkened jaw. "Touch you? You're afraid of my touch?"

"You got that right," he said, his voice raspy.

"Why?"

"Because you are trying to seduce me. I'm not seducible."

Threading his hair with her fingers, she tucked it behind his ear, then trailed her hand down his neck to his good shoulder. "You're not?"

His eyes closed as if he were in pain. "No."

"I'll tell you what. If you let me give you a bath, I'll tell you anything you want to know about me."

One eye popped open. "Anything?"

"Yes."

"Can I test this promise up front?"

"Yes."

"Have you ever given Mark a bath?"

"No."

His open eye squinted, as if he were gauging her honesty. "Okay."

Shannon's heart flipped cartwheels. She couldn't believe how much she wanted to see his naked body once more. How much she wanted to taste and smell his skin. How much she wanted to give him pleasure.

She'd explained her dilemma to a stunned Diane that afternoon at lunch. Diane had stared at her for a good long minute before saying, "Let me see if I understand you. A man—a gorgeous, sexy, virile man—is withholding sex from you because he's upset you're using him?"

"Yes," Shannon had answered glumly. "He won't even sleep in the same bed with me. He sleeps in the guest room."

"We're still talking about Rick, right? Rick Hardison, Robo-stud?"

"That's the one."

"Rick Hardison, who, before he met you, went through a woman a week?"

Shannon scowled. "A woman a week?"

"This is great, Shannon."

"A woman a week?"

Diane waved. "Pay attention. This is significant."

Shannon attempted to take her mind off the staggering statistic of Rick's womanizing. "How?"

"Don't you get it? He doesn't want you *using* him."

"I know that! That's what I've just told you."

"Do you realize this is a momentous occasion?"

"That's what I thought!" Shannon said, then lowered her voice as several nearby customers turned to glare at her. "But why?"

"Honey, you are doing to him what he and his gender have been doing to women for years. And he hates it." She laughed. "This is too precious."

"Precious as it may be, it doesn't solve my problem." She leaned forward. "I want him again," she said softly. "And he's holding out on me."

Diane tapped her fork against her lips, then her eyes lit up. "I've got two words for you."

"What?"

"Sponge bath."

Those two words had bounced through Shannon's head all day. And now that the time was near, she found the excitement of it all dizzying. She held out her hand. Rick hesitated, then engulfed her palm with his. She pulled him to his feet and led him like a little boy to the kitchen.

Only this little boy towered over her, his glorious hand warm and thrilling covering hers. In the kitchen he dutifully stopped where she pointed, in front of the chair she'd placed beside the sink.

Shannon dropped the sponge in the soapy water, then turned to him. Without asking, she tugged at his sweat pants, until they pooled at his feet. Rick stepped out of them and kicked them aside.

Deciding to leave his briefs on for now, she said, "Sit down."

Rick complied, then didn't skip a beat as he began to cross-examine her. "Do you have any brothers or sisters?"

Shannon wrung out the sponge. "Two older brothers."

"What do they do?"

She turned to him with a smile. Deciding to start on his face, she forked her fingers through the hair at his forehead and pushed it back. Then she began massaging his face. "Frank is a minister in Bethlehem, Pennsylvania. James is an engineer in Harrisburg."

When she removed the sponge from his face, she could tell from his expression that he'd enjoyed that. She wet it and wrung it out again, then started on his neck.

"Mmmmmm," he moaned. "Are your parents still living?"

"Yes. They live in Belleville. Same as me."

"Where's that?"

"Central Pennsylvania."

She washed his good shoulder, then re-wet the sponge.

"What do they do?"

"My father's a Presbyterian minister." The sponge whispered down his sculpted arm. "My mother's a Presbyterian minister's wife. And if you know anything about the life of a Presbyterian minister, you'd know that's a full-time job."

"What's it like being a minister's daughter?"

She shrugged, feeling a languor steal over her at the warm, rhythmic bathing of his body. "It's different, I guess. The rules aren't the same for a preacher's kid as they are for the rest of humanity."

"I'll bet," he said. "Especially in a small town, huh?"

Surprised by his insight, she nodded. "You get to feeling like you're under constant surveillance, and if you do anything approaching wrong or naughty, somehow your father hears about it on Sunday."

"Mmmm," he murmured, as Shannon grazed the freshly warmed sponge down his chest. "Sounds wonderful."

She stopped at his ribs. "What?"

He dropped his head back. "I would've given anything for some parental supervision." He laid his elbow on the chair back and rested his head against the wall. "I didn't get much. None in fact."

"And I got too much," Shannon mused, as she worshipped his abdomen. "We make a strange pair, don't we?"

He opened his eyes and gazed at her lazily. "Is that what this is all about, angel? Are you rebelling against your strict upbringing by having a fling with a man your parents would hate on sight?"

Shannon knelt and started washing his feet. "Maybe a little," she conceded after a moment. "But not completely." The sponge skimmed up his muscled calf. "I mean, rebellion implies flaunting your sins in their faces, don't you think?"

"And you certainly aren't going to flaunt me."

She started on the other foot. "Not because I'm ashamed of you, Rick."

"Aren't you?"

"No." She tossed the sponge in the sink, then braced her hands on his hard thighs. "In fact, I'm very flattered . . . " She kissed his rigid abdomen, inhaling the scent of soap and man. " . . . that a man as sexy as you are . . . " Slipping her fingers under the waist of his briefs, she tugged. Rick helped her by lifting his hips. " . . . is attracted to me." The proof of that attraction stood proudly before her, and Shannon grasped him.

Rick groaned. "Shannon," he said softly.

"Hmmm," she said, then took his flat nipple into her mouth.

He sucked in a breath. "You . . . you have no idea how attracted I am to you."

Her mouth moved to another part of him and Rick's body jerked. "I've . . . never wanted . . . ah, that's so good . . . anyone . . . the way I want you."

She lifted her head. "I'm glad."

"I want to be inside you, Shannon."

She stood up, smiling. While he watched with aroused, burning eyes, she lifted off her tank top, then wiggled out of her shorts and panties.

"You're so beautiful," he whispered, reaching for her.

Careful not to touch his bad shoulder or jar his tethered arm, Shannon straddled his lap. She was supremely ready for him, and she slid down on his shaft in one smooth stroke.

"Shannon," he groaned. "God, Shannon, it's never felt like this."

She rode him mindlessly, as the sweet torture built. His hand came down between their bodies, and he played her with his fingers. Shannon whimpered. No, it had never felt like this. And never would again, without Rick.

As she rode the crest to its peak, then shattered, Shannon knew that nothing and no one could make her feel like Rick could.

She cried out his name as she splintered apart.

AT THE SOUND of the knock, Rick called out, "It's open."

The door swung wide and Diane entered, carrying a couple of fast food sacks. She stopped dead when she saw him, her mouth dropping open.

Setting the lamp back down on the side table, Rick said, "What?"

"You're dusting."

He glanced at the pink feather duster, then back to Diane. "Yeah. So?"

Diane shook her head, then moved into the living room. "Hi, Bert," she said, as Bert circled her happily.

Rick chuckled. "Is that a burger in your bag, woman, or is he just happy to see you?"

Diane dropped the food on the dining table, then started pulling it out. Rick put down the duster and moved to the table. "Thanks for bringing lunch."

"Well, far be it from me to skip a meal, just because a cop calls with an S.O.S. What's the big emergency you wanted to discuss?"

"Shannon."

"What about her?" she asked, sitting.

Rick sat down too, and munched a few fries before answering. "I need some advice."

"Okay."

He tried to decide how to broach the subject. Figuring the direct approach worked best with Diane, he asked, "How much longer does Shannon have in DC?"

Diane swallowed some soda. "A couple of months. Why?"

"Is she good at her job?"

"Probably the best lab rat I've ever had. I'm going to hate to lose her."

"Then why don't you offer her a permanent position?"

The burger stopped halfway to Diane's mouth. "Because we're not her actual employer. She's on Penn State's payroll."

"So hire her away from them."

"I don't have money for another employee in my budget."

"Fire somebody."

"Rick!"

"I'm kidding. Sort of."

"You that desperate, huh?" Diane asked, eyeing him shrewdly.

He rubbed his shoulder. "I don't want her leaving DC."

"Then ask her to stay."

"She wouldn't stay just because I asked her to."

"How do you know that?"

Rick finished his burger before answering her. "She ever mention a jerk named Mark?"

Diane shrugged one shoulder as she leisurely demolished a French fry. "Once or twice."

"Is she in love with him?"

She gave him a disgusted look. "What do you think?"

"I don't know."

"Do you honestly think she's the type to play bed-roulette?"

He wiped his hands on a napkin. "No." Tossing the crumpled paper down, he added, "But I don't have any illusions, Mack. I know exactly why Shannon got involved with me."

"Why's that, Sigmund?"

"Because I'm the exact opposite of everything her parents want in a son-in-law."

Diane snorted. "She got involved with you, idiot, because she met you and was attracted to you. Just like every other woman who gets involved with a man."

He held up a finger. "But, she was attracted to me because I'm all wrong for her. So she says, at any rate."

"If you're all wrong for her, why did she come to me for advice on seducing you?"

Rick had been in the middle of sneaking Bert some fries, but at her words, he went still. Impatient, Bert nearly sucked Rick's entire hand into his mouth. "She did that?"

"She did that."

"The sponge bath was your idea?"

Diane grinned. "I might have planted the seed."

"From the bottom of my heart, I thank you."

"I take it she gives good bath?"

"She gives great bath."

"You're welcome."

Rick patted Bert, unable to look at Diane as he said, "I don't want her going home, Mack. Please help me figure out a way to make her stay."

"Well, for starters, drop the word 'make' and substitute 'convince.'"

"Done."

"As I see it," Diane said, drumming her fingers on the table, "the best way to convince her to stay is to make DC just too darn appealing."

"Meaning?"

"Court her, you dummy. Stop thinking only with your zipper and romance her."

"Oh, Lord," Rick said, rolling his eyes. He held up his fist. "We've got a couple of problems with that. One . . . " He popped up his index finger. " . . . She isn't in the least interested in being seen in public with me, and two . . ." His second finger lifted. " . . . I don't know the first thing about romancing a woman."

"You've got to be kidding me! You've managed to bed half the female population in this county!"

Rick frowned. "You're exaggerating, and don't you dare mention that to her."

Diane's gaze dropped to the table.

"What'd you tell her?" Rick growled.

"Well . . . " She waved at the unimportance of it all. "Just that your most meaningful relationships lasted seven whole days."

Rick felt his jaw go slack. "You didn't."

"It's the truth."

"I was married for almost a year!" he protested, indignant.

"Ha!" Diane scoffed. "You knew the woman two weeks before you married her, you two lived together a total of eight weeks—"

"Nine weeks and four days. Nine of the longest—"

"And the rest of your marriage was spent in court. The day your divorce was granted, you threw the biggest party DC has seen since the Obama inaugural, and you immediately entered into a meaningful relationship with Nadine Humphries which lasted three nights."

Rick sat back and crossed his good arm over his bad. "What's your point?"

"That you're a bad risk, Casanova."

"I'm a changed man."

She peered at him through slitted eyes. "Really? Truly? Because I like Shannon a whole lot and I'm not helping you break her heart."

Nodding, he said, "Really. Truly." He leaned forward. "Think about it. She and I have been together over a month and it just keeps getting better and better. I've lived under her roof four days—three days longer than I regretted living with Mary Anne—and I'm already dusting."

"There is the dusting," Diane conceded.

"And I'm doing laundry later!" he added for good measure.

"Well, that's nice, but not exactly romantic."

Rick swore. "I might have even liked Mary Anne longer if she'd done laundry once in a while. Do you know how uncomfortable dry-cleaned underwear is?"

"Well, I'm sure that men find some kind of romantic element in fabric softener, but it's not exactly a selling point for women."

"Damn. I'm doomed."

"Maybe not. Do you know how to cook?"

"Does nuking Hungry Man dinners count?"

"No. Do you know how to follow directions?"

"Never been particularly good at that."

Diane threw her hands in the air. "Are you going to work with me here, or not?"

"Will this get me Shannon?"

"No guarantees. But this will sure as hell beat washing her underwear."

"You haven't seen her underwear."

She slapped her hand on the table. "That's it. You're still a deviant. I quit."

"No, really! Please, Mack!"

After a long-suffering sigh, she said, "Okay. Get me paper and a writing instrument."

Rick got up and retrieved a notepad and pen from the kitchen. "Will this be a lot of work?"

"Yes. But it'll be worth it."

He nodded, then walked to the phone. After punching in the number, he asked to speak to Tony. "Hey, kid, want to earn some cash?"


SHANNON SIGHED as she climbed out of her car. Mentally gearing herself up to handle the scene she expected to find, she popped the trunk and retrieved the two grocery sacks.

This caretaker business was a lot of work. Especially with a partially helpless man who also didn't mind living a little slovenly.

She snorted. A little? Rick somehow managed to turn her living room into a disaster zone day after day. His partial impairment didn't stop him from making messes.

Grinning, she tossed her head. Well, he was worth it. Having his solid warmth beside her in bed at night made any extra work worthwhile. She had the feeling that she'd never get a good night's sleep again, once she left him and returned to Pennsylvania.

That thought tugged her smile down into a frown. She shook it off. For now she was here, with him, and that's all that mattered.

She struggled with the door to the kitchen. Then suddenly the knob was ripped from her hand and the door swung open. Peering between the two bags, she saw Rick, and her heart tripped over itself in its attempt to thump its way out of her chest cavity.

Definitely, the man should come with a warning label for cardiac patients. He was so tall and gorgeous and . . . wearing an apron?

That's when the smells hit her. Delicious smells. Her mouth watered, and she couldn't decide if it was the sight of Rick or the scent of roasting meat that caused it. Both, she supposed.

"Hi, angel," he said, his smile soft and alluring. He reached out with his good hand and took a grocery sack from her.

"You're wearing an apron."

"Yes."

"Are you feeling okay?" she asked, as she followed him inside. Rick dumped the one bag on the counter, then took the second from her and set it down also. Then he turned, pulled her to him and kissed her.

"I've been thinking about this all day," he said, then kissed her again. "I missed you like hell," he whispered against her neck, then kissed her again. "I want you," he breathed into her ear, then kissed her again. "Always, angel. I'll never stop wanting you."

*Welcome home,* she thought dazedly, afraid she'd puddle to the floor if he let her go. With a homecoming like this, she wouldn't care if he'd burned her house down during the day.

Before she knew what was happening, he had her blouse half unbuttoned, and his fingers traced the lace of her bra. "Damn, I love your underwear," he said.

Shivers of pleasure rippled through her. God, she didn't think she'd ever tire of this man's touch.

Then before she fully realized the importance of that thought, he'd buttoned her back up and set her away from him. "Now be a good girl and go get comfortable. I've got work to do."

Shannon opened her mouth to protest, but he'd already turned away to stir something on the stove. In a fog she took in the frilly apron strings that trailed down his back, covered his prize-winning butt and stopped at his powerful thighs.

She couldn't help herself. She giggled. Betty Crocker, he was not.

He turned back to her with a frown. "What?"

"You're cooking?"

"Well, I'm not changing the oil in the car, now am I? Of course, I'm cooking! What's wrong with that?"

"You don't know how to cook."

"Says who?"

"Says you. Last night. You didn't recognize pork chops."

He waved a wooden spoon. "I'm a reformed man." He turned her and patted her bottom. "Now go on. I can't prepare a masterpiece with you here gawking at me."

Shannon dutifully left. She took one step into the living room. And stopped. If she was gawking before, she was positively gaping now. He'd set the table and placed about a dozen candles on it. A bottle of white wine sat chilling in a silver bucket. Beside it, a bottle of red breathed.

She looked around the living room. It was spotless. Gone were the pillows, the books and magazines thrown around haphazardly, the candy bar wrappers and the half-finished cans of soda.

Shannon blinked. Were those vacuum cleaner lines in the carpet? She turned on her heel and headed back to the kitchen.

"What did you do?"

Rick finished testing a broth of some sort, then set down the spoon. "What do you mean?"

She pointed to the living room. "There are flowers in there."

"Yes. Like them?"

"And wine."

"Uh-huh."

"Candles."

"Right."

"You vacuumed."

"Yup."

"You're cooking."

"Yes."

"I repeat. What did you do?"

He swept a hand toward the living room. "I think that's obvious."

"No, I mean, what infraction are you trying to make up for?

Did you bring a woman here?"

His guilty frown tore her heart to shreds. "You did! Oh my God, you did!"

She whirled, just as a sob escaped her lips. She got two steps in before he grabbed her arm and spun her back to him. "Wait, Shannon. It's not what you think."

"You two-timing, no good, dirty, low-down—"

"I did not cheat on you!"

"—snake-bellied . . . you didn't?"

"No. All I did was ask Mack for help in romancing you."

"You did?"

He dropped her arm. "Yes, I did. And I'm completely offended that you would even *think* I'd do something like that."

"Oh, give me a break. Your reputation precedes you, Mr. Love 'Em and Leave 'Em."

His fist hit his hip. "Between the two of us, angel," he said in a menacing growl, "I'm not the one cheating on my boyfriend."

A blush raced up her throat to her cheeks. "He's not my boyfriend, anymore."

"Is that right? When did you come to that conclusion?"

She bit her lip. "Recently."

"Has he been informed of your change in plans?"

"Not yet."

"Terrific. So you can change your mind again, if you want to."

Shaking her head vehemently, she said, "I can't marry him. Not now."

"Marry him? Marry him? He's asked you to marry him?"

"Well, yes, but—"

"You weren't cheating on your boyfriend! You were cheating on your fiancé!"

"No! I—"

"Let me tell you something, doll. You are not marrying him."

"That's what I just—"

"If you think I'm going to stand by and let you marry this

guy, you are crazy."

He blustered on for another minute or so, and Shannon tried not to burst out laughing. Having a big, dumb cop shouting at her while he wore a gingham apron that said Mifflin County Bean Soup Festival was just a little too funny.

"Are you quite finished?" she asked, when his ranting sputtered to a halt.

"I think so."

"For your information, Mr. Hardison, I never agreed to marry him. And technically I never cheated, because our agreement was to see other people if we wanted to."

"Has he been seeing other people?"

Her lips pursed. "I don't think so."

"Well, you sure as hell have been. You've seen a whole lot of me and you're going to see a whole lot more."

"Oh, goodie."

That brought him up short. "Oh, goodie?"

"Goodie, goodie, goodie." She skimmed her palm up his arm. "Can I see a whole lot more right now?"

He swallowed. "Uh, I'd love to, but I have a dinner to prepare."

"To hell with dinner."

"But—"

She backed up a step and pulled her blouse from her skirt. "Well, if you're not interested, I'll just go get . . . comfortable."

His eyes followed her fingers as they unbuttoned her blouse. "Aren't you hungry?"

"Oh, yes."

She shrugged out of her shirt, then unbuttoned her skirt and let it fall to the floor. The struggle on his face was hysterical. God, the man was one big hormone. She loved that about him.

She shimmied out of her half-slip. "Well, I guess you better get back to work." Turning, she headed out of the kitchen.

They made it as far as the living room.

# Chapter Nine

"TA-DA!"

"Oh, Rick!" Shannon cried, dropping her purse on the kitchen table.

She touched his untethered arm, admired his chest—bare but for a small bandage right below his collar bone.

Though she was thrilled for him, it was a bittersweet victory. Now they had no excuses whatsoever for him to stay with her.

He'd been living with her for six weeks, although, in truth, he probably could have done just fine on his own after the first week. But somehow they'd eased into a routine that they'd both found comfortable.

Well, not comfortable exactly. At least not for Shannon. Because there was an edge to their living arrangement, too. She anticipated coming home like she never had in her life. Knowing this sexy, sensual man would be waiting for her always had her breaking speed limits to get there.

And she never knew from one day to the next what she'd find when she arrived. Rick was full of surprises. Champagne and a bubble bath one night, a picnic in the back yard the next.

One night two weeks ago, she'd come home to no Rick at all. Stunned and frightened, she'd collapsed on the couch and cried. That's how he'd found her when he returned, delayed at the D.A.'s office as he'd prepared to testify against some drug runners.

"Shannon? What's wrong, angel?" he'd asked, gathering her in his arm and pressing her face to his chest.

She'd snuffled. "I thought . . . I thought you were gone."

"Well, technically, I was. I had to prepare for court tomorrow."

"I mean . . . gone . . . for good."

He'd chuckled softly. "Ah, angel, you can't get rid of me that easily. I still need lots of TLC."

"No, you don't. You're back at work and you're getting physical therapy. You don't really even need that sling anymore, and besides, I've never known anyone who could accomplish as much as you do with just one hand." She'd rubbed her nose. "You don't . . . need me anymore."

"That's where you're wrong, sweetheart. I need you a great deal."

"You're just being nice. You do more around here than I do. You could do just fine at your own place."

"Are you kicking us out?"

"No!" she'd said, and raised her head. "Please, not yet. Please wait until . . . until the sling's off for good."

"Until the sling's off for good," he'd agreed.

And the sling was now off for good. It was over. Finally over for good. She didn't have one excuse left to keep him with her.

"I'm . . . so . . . ha . . . hap . . . happy for you," she managed, before wheeling around and racing to her bedroom.

Of course he followed her. "Shannon?"

Plucking a pillow from under the comforter, she hugged it to her, against the rending chasm in her belly that threatened to rip her in two.

"Shannon?"

"Yes?" she whispered, not able to meet his gaze.

"What's wrong?"

"Nothing. Everything's peachy. You're fully recovered, and there's not a reason on earth for you to stay here with me. So . . . so . . . goodbye."

He tore the pillow from her and dragged her to her feet. "Just like that, huh?"

She tipped her head back and gazed up at him, her heart pumping painfully. "That was our agreement."

"True," he said, nodding. "But right now I feel like celebrating. And who better to celebrate with than the woman who nursed me back to health?"

Shannon's pulse jumped, and something akin to hope bloomed in her. "Celebrate?"

"Uh-huh. Celebrate."

"How?"

"Well, now, I did a little shopping today. I've got a meal planned that's going to blow you away." He held up his hands and wiggled his fingers. "I'm going to feed you. Every bite. With my two good hands."

"That . . . sounds wonderful." It sounded more than wonderful. It sounded sensual as heck.

"One more night, Shannon. That's all I'm asking for. One more night."

"One more," she agreed.

He grinned. She sure would miss that grin. And his company. She would miss his company terribly. She'd come to love the quiet times, at night, when they took turns making supper, or actually prepared it together.

She'd learned so much about her dream lover in the last six weeks. All of it wonderful. She didn't think she'd ever admired a man more.

Occasionally Tony would come to dinner. She loved sitting back and watching Rick with Tony. He had a way with kids, she'd realized. He taught Tony by example, and Tony seemed to blossom and grow under his tutelage. Tony was a lucky young man. It seemed he would have Rick's friendship forever.

She, on the other hand, had only one more night. Then it was back to Plan A. She was really, really beginning to hate Plan A.

Rick kissed her. She melted against him, loving the hard muscle and sinew that lay under the smooth and surprisingly soft skin of his chest. And his scent. As long as she lived, she would always associate male power and appeal with the smell of Rick's flesh.

He lifted his head, his smile full of promise. "You know what I'm looking forward to most?"

Shannon shook her head slowly. "No," she whispered.

"What?"

"I look forward to re-learning the missionary position. I look forward to laying on top of you, being inside you, touching you with both hands, kissing you, and watching your face. God, I'd never thought I'd be so excited to try the missionary position."

He took her hand and started to pull her toward the door. "Come on, let's start on dinner. You're going to be dazzled by my talent."

"Rick?" she said, digging in her heels.

He turned back to her. "Hmmm?"

"About that missionary position?"

He shot her a lazy, smoky smile. "Yes?"

"How about if we hold off dinner until we re-acquaint ourselves with it?"


"YOU ARE BEAUTIFUL by candlelight," Rick said, then sipped some wine. He set down his goblet and picked up a piece of lobster and dipped it in clarified butter. He held it up to her lips.

Shannon opened her mouth, but instead of feeding it to her, Rick traced her lips with it. "Of course, you're beautiful in any light," he whispered, then popped the delicate meat into her mouth.

Considering Shannon was busy savoring the lobster and butter, she couldn't reply right away. But she sure could return the sentiment. Candlelight emphasized the beauty of the beast sitting beside her.

The play of shadows emphasized the planes of his face, making him appear at once dangerous and ethereal. That was Rick, she thought in a burst of insight. He was a mass of contradictions, both ends of the spectrum.

He was a powerful man, with a touch so gentle sometimes it made her want to cry. He'd survived an unspeakable childhood, and now he fought against the very environment that had shaped him. He could transform from a nasty-looking thug to a romance cover model with just a smile, a tuck of his hair behind his ears. He could testify coldly, succinctly, graphically in court about the most heinous of crimes, then come home and play with his dog on the floor.

He was both everything and nothing she wanted in a man.

Shannon swallowed the sweet lobster meat, then accepted the plump grape he offered her, nibbling at his fingers. "You were incredible in court today."

He lifted a shoulder. "Standard stuff."

"Standard? Ha, I don't think so. I don't think I've ever heard a detective call a defense lawyer a swine before and get away with it."

"I didn't get away with it," he protested. "I got fined fifty bucks for contempt."

"The judge was laughing when he fined you. And fifty dollars is a slap on the wrist."

Rick fed her some cheese, then held her goblet up for her to drink. "Why'd you come, anyway? You didn't handle the scientific testing in that case."

A flush of heat warmed her face. "I . . . was just curious to see you in action. And to see how you looked in a suit."

He wrinkled his nose and picked up his wine glass. "Uncomfortable."

"Oh, no! You looked wonderful. Like you were born to wear one."

The goblet hit the table. "Make no mistake, Shannon. I was not born to wear a suit. I wear them in court because it's department policy."

He tossed a piece of cheese to Bert, seeming suddenly agitated. Shannon had come to expect that reaction from Rick, though she wasn't certain she understood its source. Why did the thought of looking respectable bother him so much?

She accepted more lobster, cheese and fruit from his fingers, and fed him in turn, mulling over the man. What drove him? What mattered to him? Most importantly, why did she care?

When she couldn't take any more, she held up her hand. "I'm stuffed."

Rick grinned and wiped his fingers with a napkin. "Did you like that?"

"Oh, yes. The presentation as much as the substance."

"Good."

They both sat back in their chairs, just sipping wine quietly and gazing at each other. A need to know him, the man underneath, welled up in Shannon. "How old were you when you went to live with your grandfather?" she blurted.

Rick's head jerked back in surprise. For a moment he didn't look like he'd answer her, then a lopsided grin appeared on his face. "When I was fifteen."

"Fifteen? But I thought I heard you tell Tony your parents died when you were younger than he is?"

"They did. I was twelve when they died."

"Then where'd you live for those three years?"

He shrugged. "Sometimes at friends' houses. Sometimes in abandoned cars. Sometimes in abandoned buildings."

"Rick, no!" she breathed. "Why? Didn't your grandfather want you? And where was child services? My God, you were a baby—"

He held up a hand. "Whoa! Slow down." Looking down, he turned her hand over and started tracing circles on her wrist with his thumb. "When my parents died, child services did get involved. I was sent to a foster home." He looked up. "I was never a baby, Shannon. I was never a child. I never had that opportunity. As far back as I can remember, I was on my own."

He took a noisy breath. "So you can imagine my shock when I was sent to live with this family. Suddenly I was being told what time I had to go to bed, who I could be friends with, when to do my homework. I didn't take it well. I ran away and never looked back."

"But surely child services went looking for you."

"If they did, they never found me. I have the sneaking suspicion that the family had already considered me a lost cause. I have the feeling they never reported my disappearance. I'm assuming they figured they'd be notified if my body ever showed up somewhere, and that would be the end of the money they received for me."

"My God! But wouldn't the school get involved when you stopped going?"

He looked at her curiously. "I didn't stop going to school."

"You didn't?"

"Hell, no. Call me strange, but I enjoyed school. It beat the hell out of wandering the streets. And it was a lot warmer in winter, too."

"How did you fall through the cracks of the system?"

"Don't know. Don't care. I survived."

"What . . . what did you do for food? For clothes?"

"What does anyone do? I worked. After school and on weekends I worked under the table as a bike messenger."

She lowered her fork, put her elbows on the table and rested her head on her intertwined hands. "Let me get this straight. You were a homeless kid, but you still went to school and you worked."

"That's about it."

"That's remarkable."

His eyebrows arrowed downward. "Not really. And don't get that moony look on your face, angel. I was no saint. I got into my share of trouble. In fact, it was after I got picked up for . . . hmmm, borrowing a car that my grandfather finally caught up with me."

"Borrowing?"

"I was going to return it!" he defended. "I just needed wheels to get my friend's stupid little brother to a hospital. The idiot got hold of some bad acid."

Fascinated, Shannon asked, "So what happened?"

"I got sent to juvie hall. My grandfather found out and he used his influence to get my time there reduced, on the condition that he take complete custody." He swirled his wine. "He was a funny old goat."

"You loved him."

"I hated his guts. At least at first." He poured them both more wine. "I blamed him for what my father had become."

"Which was?"

"A spoiled rich man's son whose only concern in the world was self-gratification. My grandfather bailed him out every time he got himself in trouble. He didn't give a damn about anyone or anything except money. He and my mother suited each other perfectly."

"How'd they die, Rick?"

"They were shot by some gang members when my father refused to hand over his wallet." He shook his head. "The irony still floors me. He lived for money, and he died for it, too."

"And when your grandfather found you?"

He laughed, a sound just tinged with bitterness. "He literally imprisoned me in that mausoleum of his. All I did was defy him. I kept trying to run away, but he'd hired these thugs to follow me. One night he literally tied me to the dining room chair to keep me there long enough to hear him out."

"What did he say?"

"Basically, he said, 'I screwed up with my own son, and I'm not going to make that mistake twice. And damn if I'm going to let you throw your life away, boy. Do you really want to follow in your father's footsteps? Damn if I didn't think I spotted a lot more spine in you than that.'"

"Oh, Rick!"

"I fought him. Every step of the way. Then the old codger got smart on me. He started taunting me, laughing at me every time I made what he called a 'loser' move. Whenever I stumbled, he just smiled like he expected it from me. He got me so damn mad that I vowed I was going to prove to him that I wasn't a loser. I became a little crazy, even. Started handing out vigilante justice at school and on the streets. I became what is known as a gangbuster."

Rick seemed lost in thought, in a time and place that obviously marked a turning point for him. This was the most he'd ever revealed to her, and Shannon was enthralled. "So, what happened?"

"I got carried away one time. A fifteen year old pregnant girl got caught in a gang shootout. I hunted down the gunman and beat him to a pulp. The authorities wanted to charge me with aggravated assault and attempted murder, but the creep recovered, and refused to point to me as his attacker, even though everyone knew it had been me.

"My grandfather was livid. He pointed out that I wasn't going to do the world much good behind bars. He said, 'I understand your passion, boy, but you haven't got the brains God gave a moth. You're asking to go up in flames. If you're so hellfire bent on ridding the world of drugs, join the system, don't fight it. Become a cop. Or a lawyer. Someone who makes a difference.'"

Rick shook his head. "I explained in quite colorful terms exactly what I thought of lawyers, and that being a police officer wasn't exactly a prestigious job that would make my grandpappy proud." Rick lifted his gaze, his eyes blazing into hers with an emotion she couldn't identify. "He said, 'The prestige is in being good at it.'"

Shannon sucked in a breath. "Oh, Rick! And you are! Believe me, I've heard plenty about your reputation. You're a wonderful cop."

"I don't know if I'd go that far," he said quietly. "But I do think I'm making a small difference. I hope so, anyway." He smiled. "Anyway, the next night my grandfather brought home this man for dinner. He was a cop. And one of the most decent, passionate human beings I've ever met. We sat up all night talking about his job. By the time he left, I knew what I wanted to do with the rest of my life.

"I thank God every day that my grandfather lived long enough to see me make detective. You wouldn't believe the pride in his eyes when I told him. That's when I realized that he'd saved my life."

By this time, Shannon's eyes had misted, and she blinked back the tears. "That's an incredible story."

His hands lifted helplessly. "I got lucky. For every one of me, there are hundreds of kids out there who don't have grandfathers who give a damn."

"Is that why you care about Tony so much?"

He frowned. "Who said I cared about the kid? He's a

mouthy little punk."

Shannon pursed her lips to keep from grinning. "Oh, yes, you just tolerate him, right?"

"That's right, angel."

"Is that why you bribed him to try out for the team?"

Rick's frown turned into an out-and-out scowl. "I just don't want to have to bother busting the kid sometime in the future. I'm saving myself the trouble."

"Right."

Looking suddenly uncomfortable, Rick shot to his feet and pulled a quarter from his jeans pocket. Flipping it, he said, "Your call."

"Heads."

He slapped it on the back of his hand, then showed it to her. "Tails. You wash, I dry."

Shannon stuck her tongue out at him, standing and gathering dishes.

Rick grinned and his tense shoulders seemed to relax. "Watch it, angel, or I'll find lots more uses for that pretty little tongue of yours."

Shannon's heart fluttered. "I'm counting on it, cowboy."


RICK HUMMED an old Willie Nelson tune while he returned pots and pans to their proper cabinets. The casual ease he displayed for Shannon was in sharp contrast to the inner turmoil churning through him.

This was it. Their last night. Tomorrow morning he would pack his and Bert's possessions and cart them back to his empty house. Life would return to normal—his self-imposed solitude restored.

So why did he feel so damn lousy about it all?

He should be content to move on. After all, he'd found in the last weeks he'd lived with Shannon that the burning fire in their physical relationship had waned slightly. They no longer spent every moment in bed, taking turns driving each other wild.

Now, on many nights they didn't actually hit the sheets until midnight, Shannon's usual bedtime. On those nights they spent playing games or watching TV or just talking. He no longer felt the urge to possess her body constantly. He was content to just have her company instead.

Which obviously meant that he was finally reaching saturation point. A good thing, really. Well, it wasn't like he didn't still want her. He did. He still found their sex life mind-blowing. He just found other things he liked doing with her, too.

Problem was, he felt pretty certain that their affair wouldn't entirely end with his move back to his own house. He was pretty sure she'd still like to get together occasionally, before she moved back to Pennsylvania. But with his physical removal from her house, the close camaraderie would be gone.

They'd revert to being mere lovers again. It was the friendship that would disappear, along with his personal items from her house.

He should be glad.

He was miserable.

A clap of thunder made them both jump. Rick moved to the kitchen window. "Uh-oh. I hung laundry out there this afternoon."

He started for the door, but Shannon stopped him. "I'll get it. You finish drying, Mr. Clean."

He swatted her butt with the dish towel as she sailed past him. Bending over, she grabbed the laundry basket from beside the door. Rick admired the view. He sure would miss sights like that.

Reluctantly he returned to putting away dishes. Just as he finished, the phone rang.

He threw the drying towel on the counter and grabbed the receiver. "Yeah?"

Silence.

"Hello?" he said.

"I . . . must have the wrong number," a man said.

"Who you looking for?"

"Uh . . . Shannon . . . Shannon Walsh."

Rick froze. "Who's calling?" he asked, trying, and failing, to keep his voice from sounding like sandpaper scraping along the phone line.

"Mark Hunter. Is this Shannon's number?"

"Yeah." Rick considered "accidentally" disconnecting. In the end, he just said, "Hold on."

Stalking to the back door, he flung it open. "Phone!" he barked across the lawn.

Shannon nearly leapt over the clothes line. She turned to Rick with her hand over her heart. "Who is it?"

Since Rick didn't want the pansy to hear him, he closed the door and stomped down the steps toward her. "It's loverboy."

"Oh!" Shannon looked from him to the clothes helplessly.

"I'll finish this," he said, swiping a violet teddy from her hands. "Go."

She hesitated.

"Go!"

She ran to the door. If he wasn't so pissed off, he might have appreciated the sight. Instead he quelled a real strong desire to tear all her lingerie to shreds, just so Mark Hunter would never have the pleasure of seeing her wearing them.

He finished folding all of the clothes, then trudged back to the house, praying she'd finished the conversation. He opened the door quietly and looked in through the screen.

What he saw nearly splintered his heart. Shannon sat at the kitchen table, stroking Bert with one hand, swatting tears from her eyes with the other.

Torn, Rick dumped the clothes basket and went to her, taking her arms and hauling her to her feet. "What? What happened?"

Those pools of blue couldn't even lift higher than his abdomen. "It's . . . over."

"What's over?"

"Mark . . . and me."

She didn't sound happy. In fact, she sounded miserable. Her sniffling echoed through the room, and Rick had no idea how to deal with it, because he wasn't certain of the cause.

"You told him?" he ventured. "About us?"

She shook her head pitifully. "I didn't have to. He called to ask me if I'd mind if he took Jean Waters to the Grange Fair."

"What did you tell him?"

"I . . . told him he could see anyone he wanted to."

"And?" he prodded.

"Then he asked me what was going to happen when I got home."

"And?"

"And . . . and I asked . . . if we couldn't wait until I got home to discuss it."

"And?"

"And . . . he said . . . if I was going to break up with him, he wanted to know now, so . . . so he felt free to date."

"And?"

"And . . . I told him . . . to feel free to date."

"And?"

"And . . . he was quiet for a minute, then he said, 'I see.'" She nearly wailed the last word.

"Why are you so upset? I thought that was what you wanted."

She looked up, startled, her eyes shimmering with tears. "It was just . . . sad. I mean, we were together three years, Rick. I never wanted to hurt him."

Rick pulled her into his arms. "No, I know you didn't. I'm sorry."

"It . . . just seemed . . . like an awful way to end it."

"I know."

She sobbed quietly against his chest for he didn't know how long. She clutched at his T-shirt convulsively, and her tears soon soaked through to moisten his skin. When she was finally spent, she heaved a deep sigh, then pulled back. "I'm sorry."

He brushed away a few remaining tears with his thumb. "You'd be a pretty cold woman if you didn't feel awful. Nothing to be sorry about."

Her smile trembled. "Thanks for understanding."

He returned her smile. He had an overwhelming urge to take her to bed and make her forget all about her problems, but he didn't think that was a very good idea at the moment. So he led her back to the living room, turned on the CD player and put in the first CD he could grab, Chopin.

As the soothing music filled the room, he wrapped his arms around her and started swaying with the melody. Shannon followed his lead, her hiccups slowing, then stopping altogether.

Rick stroked one hand through her hair, inhaling the alluring, clean scent of it. So many things about her he was going to miss like hell. Even something so stupid as the smell of her shampoo.

And then there were the important things he'd miss. Like the feel of her hands on his body. Right now she was skimming them up and down his back.

He kissed her cheek, then her temple, then each damp eyelid in turn. Shannon made soft gaspy sounds that ricocheted right through his body. He'd miss the sounds she made when she was aroused most of all.

He was going to miss her.

Terribly.

"Shannon?"

"Hmmm?"

"Have I been a real pain to have around?"

Her eyelids fluttered open. "No," she said softly. "I've really lo . . . liked having you here."

He swallowed and screwed up his courage. "So . . . why don't I stay?"

Her head sank back as she stared up at him with those big, expressive eyes. "What?"

He tried to shrug casually, but his heart was working furiously. "Since you're only going to be in town for a few more weeks, and since we both enjoy the arrangement, I thought—" He cleared his dry throat. "—that we might as well enjoy the time you have left here." Pressing her head to his chest, so he didn't have to witness her expression, he added, "Together."

She took a long time answering him. While Rick waited, he held his breath.

"That . . . would be great."

His breath whooshed out. "Does that mean I can stay? Here? With you?"

Her head pushed against his hand, so he released it. She looked up, and the emotion in her eyes appeared very positive to him. Almost . . . joyful. "Does Bert come with the deal?"

Hearing his name, Bert perked up.

Incapable of hiding a stupid grin, Rick asked, "Depends on whether he's a liability or an asset."

Shannon seemed to ponder that. Looking over her shoulder at Bert, she said, "Stay!"

Bert bounded over to them, nosing his way between their bodies. Shannon scruffed between his ears, then bent and kissed his nose. Bert looked like he wanted to hyperventilate with happiness.

Rick couldn't blame him, but he wanted this settled. He scratched his dog, then said, "Come!"

Bert managed an Academy Award winning performance of a dog wronged, turning his head away and whimpered. Then he sidled to the corner and slunk down.

"You hurt his feelings!" Shannon accused.

Rick snorted. "Step aside, Lassie."

"But—" She started to pull away from him.

He grabbed her right back. "No. This is human talk right now. Do you . . . " He dragged the pad of his finger from her chin to the pulsepoint of her throat. " . . . want me to stay, or not?"

"I want you to stay."

"For as long as you're here?"

"Yes," she breathed.

"What if you end up staying forever?"

"Oh, I can't! I have obligations to Penn State! I have a paper to write, lectures to give, obligations to—"

Silencing her with a kiss, he submitted to taking what he could get. "Fine. Just until you go home, then."

"Just until I go home."

"And until you go home, you're mine, Shannon."

"Well, I'm not sure I'm comfortable—"

"Tell me you're mine. For the time we have left, tell me you're mine."

She made that breathy sound again, the one that drove him crazy. "I'm yours. While I'm here, I'm yours."

"Tell me you love me."

Her gasp of surprise couldn't rival the zing of utter shock that flashed through him like a lightning bolt. He had no idea where that had come from. None, whatsoever. But, no matter, he couldn't stop himself. "Tell me. Say it to me. I know you won't mean it, Shannon, but for some reason, I want to see your lips form those words. And I want them directed at me. Just once."

Shannon stared at Rick in mute shock. She had no idea how to handle this. Her heart was doing aerobics and her stomach had a butterfly collection that would have thrilled a lepidopterist. "It . . . I . . . would be lying."

"Lie to me."

"I—"

"Say it."

"I . . . love you."

His hands tensed on her shoulder blades. "Say it again."

"I LOVE YOU," she whispered, wondering why it slid off her lips so easily.

"Say it, Shannon. I'm going to make love to you, and I want to hear you say it the whole time."

His eyes flamed with a passion that almost scared her. If she didn't trust him so much, she'd stop this insanity.

He tore her blouse straight off, then pushed down her camisole, baring her upper body. "Say, it, dammit."

His mouth covered her breast and Shannon wanted to die it felt so good. "I love you."

Before she knew it, he'd stripped her naked, making her say those words every time he revealed more of her flesh. Each time she said it, it came easier. As she slipped into blissful oblivion, she began to chant the words. They became a mantra that added untold pleasure to their lovemaking. Every time she uttered them, Rick seemed to go more wild, until she didn't know an inch of herself that he didn't possess.

"I love you, Rick," she gasped, right before her climax snatched her from earth. Everything inside her burst free. She felt like a firework, hurtling colorful sparks through the sky.

As he exploded inside her, she didn't know whether she heard or imagined Rick groan, "I love you so much, angel."

# Chapter Ten

SHANNON RESTED her head against Rick's shoulder, trying to sort out the conflicting emotions racing through her. They were still sprawled on the living room floor, still exhausted from their tumultuous lovemaking moments ago.

They'd made love so many times in the last couple of months, but never so desperately, so stirringly. Something had changed.

What?

Was it just a matter of uttering those three magic words? How could that be, when the words were a lie? She didn't love Rick. She couldn't love Rick. Their relationship was destined to end, and Shannon didn't want to return to Pennsylvania nursing a broken heart.

So why had he demanded they exchange the sentiment? And why had the sound of Rick proclaiming his love set her heart and body on fire? Making love with Rick was always a wonderfully satisfying experience. She'd lay odds he was probably the world's most generous lover. But tonight . . . tonight . . .

The surge of emotion that pulsed through her frightened her. She gripped Rick's waist more tightly, curling her fingers into his heated, damp flesh.

"What, angel?" he asked quietly, laying his hand over hers.

"I . . . I'm confused."

All was silent for several moments, save for Shannon's ragged breathing, rattling in her ears.

"About what?" he asked finally.

Shannon lifted her head and stared down at him. "That was . . . different." Her gaze skittered to his throat. "Did . . . you feel it, too?"

He took a deep breath, his chest swelling, then relaxing. "I felt it."

"What . . . what happened just now?" She worked up the courage to look him in the eye. "What happened, Rick?"

His smile was slow in coming. He reached up and pushed a curl from her cheek, letting his fingers linger on her face. "I don't think you want to hear my opinion on the matter."

"Oh, but I do!" She released his waist and let her fingers trail up his body, until she touched them to his lips. "Tell me what just happened to me . . . to us."

He hesitated. "I think we just—"

The jangle of the phone interrupted him. Rick uttered an oath. "Don't answer that."

Shannon smiled, even as she pulled away. "Have to. I'm on call tonight."

She got up and walked to the phone, acutely aware of Rick's gaze on her naked body. "Hello?"

"Shannon?"

Shannon cringed at the sound of her mother's voice. She'd give anything to have taken back the last few seconds and let the answering machine pick up. Silently she decided to sign up for call screening. "Hi, Mother."

"Well, I must say I'm relieved you answered your own phone."

"Excuse me?"

"Mark tells me a man answered your phone earlier this evening."

Oh, no! She eyed Rick, who'd stood up and started gathering their clothes. He handed her her camisole and panties, then shrugged ruefully at the torn blouse.

"Yes, well, a friend was here for dinner."

Rick frowned.

"What friend is this?"

"Just . . . a neighbor."

Rick's frown deepened. With jerky movements, he donned his t-shirt, then his briefs and jeans.

There was a long, screaming silence on the other end of the

phone. Finally her mother said, "What's going on down there, Shannon? You've been acting very strange the last couple of weeks. And now this . . . this rift in your relationship with Mark."

Taking a breath for courage, Shannon said, "It's not just a rift, Mother. Mark and I are finished."

"How could you do this, Shannon? Do you have any idea what a fine catch Mark is?"

Oh, yes, she knew what a fine catch Mark was. How could she not, when her parents kept reminding her?

Her mother decided to remind her one more time. "Why, he's probably the most sought after bachelor in town. He's the most respected large animal veterinarian in three counties, Shannon. His reputation is beyond reproach. And—"

"He's one of the largest contributors to the church," Shannon finished for her.

The silence vibrated with shock, and not only her mother's. Shannon couldn't believe her impertinence. She shimmied into her panties and camisole, waiting for the reproach that was sure to come.

Amazingly, when her mother spoke again, she didn't sound angry. Only slightly bewildered. "What's gotten into you, Shannon?"

"I . . . guess I'm just . . . tired."

"Tell me about this man who came to dinner."

Shannon's gaze flew to Rick, who lounged casually on the couch, watching her. "There's nothing to tell, mother."

"Are you dating him?"

She turned her back on Rick. "No. Please, mother. He's . . . it's nothing."

She winced when she heard Rick let out a disgusted grunt. What did he expect? Did he want her to confess to her mother that she had a lover living under her roof? That would win her a record-setting visit from her mother.

"I'm coming for a visit."

Shannon's jaw came unhinged. "What?" she whispered.

"I'm coming down there. I want to see for myself that

you're all right."

"That's not necessary, Mother. Really, I'm fine. And I'll be home in a few weeks."

"No, I've made up my mind. I'm coming first thing tomorrow. I'll have to find someone to take my place at Bridge Club, but that shouldn't be too much of a problem."

Shannon searched desperately for an excuse to keep her mother in Pennsylvania, but nothing came to mind. The more she protested, the more determined her mother would be to see for herself what was going on.

Suddenly she felt ten years old again. And it made her so angry inside. She was an adult, for God's sake. When were her parents going to let her grow up?

But she didn't have the fight in her now. She was too confused by all that had happened that day. That day? More like that summer. Ever since she'd set eyes on the man idling on her couch, her life had turned upside down.

She sighed. "Well, I think it's a wasted trip, but certainly I'd love to see you."

"Well, fine. Give me directions."

With a dreaded, sick feeling inside, Shannon gave her mother directions on how to program the GPS. She avoided Rick's eyes while she did so.

When she finally hung up, she leaned on the table, fighting nausea. Then resolutely, she turned to him. "You have to leave."

Rick gazed at her blandly. "Mom's coming for a visit, is she?"

"Yes."

He stood up and strolled to her. Shannon drank in his stride, his form, his features. God, she was going to miss him. "It's just for a couple of days, I'm sure. Then . . . then you can come back."

He gazed at her for a moment, and Shannon had a tough time meeting his eye straight on. "All right," he said finally. "I'd like to meet your mother, though. How about if I take the two of you out to dinner one night?"

Her reaction was swift and instinctive. "No!" When his eyes

narrowed, she laid a palm on his forearm. "Please understand, Rick. My mother . . . well, she's very old-fashioned. She . . . " Shannon shivered as his features set in a cold, grim line. "She just wouldn't understand . . . you."

"I see."

Unfortunately his tone and his near sneer told her he saw too well. "I . . . just as soon as she leaves, I'll call you."

"Don't bother."

"Wh . . . why?"

She knew the answer before it left his lips, but still it ripped through her. "I'm not coming back, Shannon."

"Please," she whispered. "Please understand."

He stared at her, then just shook his head. "You know, for a little while there—just a little while—I actually allowed myself to believe you cared about me, even if you didn't realize it, yet." He waved at the phone. "That just proves how stupid I was. I thought forcing you to say the words would make them come true. Really, really stupid, huh?"

Without another word, he walked around her and headed down the hall.

Shannon dogged his steps. "Rick, wait!"

Grabbing his backpack from the bedroom, he brushed her aside and stalked to the bathroom, the anger leaving a trail of steam in his wake.

Shannon cornered him. "How can I make you understand?"

"Understand what? That you're ashamed of me? That I'm not good enough to be introduced to your family?"

"It's not that, it's just . . . " Words failed her.

Rick leaned his hip against the counter and crossed his arms. "I'm waiting."

"I just . . . don't want to create waves."

With a snort, Rick returned to stuffing his toiletries into the pack. When he finished, he pushed her aside and left the bathroom.

Shannon chased him down the hall, wanting to scream, beg, cry. Passing through the living room, Rick whistled for Bert. At the kitchen door, he turned around and swept his gaze over her one final time.

"Rick," she breathed. "Please, don't leave this way."

"Grow up, Shannon."

Those three words were like a slap on the face. A very well-deserved slap. Tears pooled in her eyes and her shoulders slumped. "Will I . . . ever see you again?"

"Not bloody likely." He turned toward the door, then back to her. "You just don't get it, do you, angel?"

"Get what?"

"You know what's really funny? I actually meant it when I told you I loved you. Unlike you, I wasn't lying."

"Oh, Rick!"

"I do love you, Shannon. But for the life of me I can't figure out why."

"I . . . love you, too."

He shook his head, his expression bleak. "You can stop lying, angel. I don't want to hear empty words anymore."

"But—"

He ignored her, turning his attention to Bert. "Stay!"

Bert looked from Rick to Shannon. Her throat ached, and the tears started streaming down her cheeks. "Stay," she choked out.

Head hanging low, Bert followed Rick out the door. What Shannon couldn't manage to say was that she'd meant that word for Rick, not Bert.


"MACKENZIE," Diane said into her office phone.

"Fletcher," Tom answered back.

Diane sat back in her chair. "How's it hanging, GQ?"

Tom gave her a succinct, two word description of how it was going. "If the man doesn't get himself killed soon, I might have to murder him myself."

Diane shook her head. "He's still acting nutty?"

"Nutty? He's acting like a freaking maniac! He's storming gang hangouts like he's Superman and he's pissing off a lot of very shady characters." Tom blew out a frustrated-sounding breath. "How are things in your neighborhood?"

Leaning back, Diane glanced out her office door into the lab. Shannon was busy staring into a microscope, but Diane knew what she'd see if Shannon looked up. Red-rimmed, tired, haunted eyes. "About the same. She looks like someone just murdered her puppy."

"This is out of control. We have to do something."

"What do you suggest, Dr. Ruth?"

"Intervention."

"Excuse me?" Diane asked.

"I say we kidnap the two of them, lock them in a room and force them to talk to each other."

"Bad idea. First of all, Shannon's mother's in town. Second of all, you know your partner better than that. The more we push him toward her, the more he'll pull away."

"True," Fletch admitted glumly. "So you have any better ideas?"

"Hmmm. Maybe."

"What?"

"Let's work on them separately." She took her mechanical pencil from behind her ear and tapped it on the desk. "How about if we show them what they're missing by giving them what they want?"

"Huh?"

"You up for a little play-acting?"

"Mack, I'm up for a little bomb-detonating if it'll get me my partner back."

"Okay, here's the deal. A double date."

"With Hardison and Shannon?"

"With Hardison and a woman who will appreciate him. Thoroughly. Completely. Utterly."

"I don't get it."

"You will."

"If this works, I will be thoroughly, completely, utterly grateful."

"I'll find a way for you to make it up to me. Now, here's what I want you to do . . ."

SHANNON GLANCED up when the door to the reception area buzzed to admit someone. Her heart started galloping when she spotted Tom Fletcher. Holding her breath, she waited to see if his partner was with him.

Obviously, he wasn't.

Tom smiled and waved, but he knew better than to come too close while she was handling evidence.

Shannon thought she managed to smile back, but she couldn't be sure. She looked down as she jelled the slides, but then her gaze drifted back to Tom, who headed directly for Diane's office.

Shannon's eyes nearly bugged out when she saw him lean over Diane and kiss her. Long and lingering, it was not a polite, friendly kiss.

When had Diane and Tom started dating? Shannon felt a little irritated that Diane hadn't shared this little piece of monumental events. After all, she'd confided all kinds of details about her relationship with Rick. Or lack thereof.

The work station Shannon was using this afternoon sat only a few yards from Diane's office, and she had no trouble hearing their conversation. Not like she was eavesdropping, but they weren't exactly trying to keep their voices down.

"You look good enough to eat, sweetcakes," Tom said.

"Why, thanks, sugarplum! You too."

Sugarplum?

"So, are we all set for tonight?"

Diane seemed to hesitate. "Yes, but I'm still not sure about this, honey pie."

"Trust me, it's just what my partner needs."

Shannon's head came up and she went still.

"But, so soon? I know their split was a mutual decision, but are you sure he's really up to dating already?"

Tom snorted. "We are talking about my partner, aren't we?"

"True. Still, Shannon—"

"—dumped him." Tom said flatly. "And not for the first time." He lowered his voice, so that Shannon had to strain to hear him. "Look, I really like her, and I know she's your friend, but I also know my partner, and what he needs right now is a little diversion."

"Well, all right, if you say so, cupcake."

Cupcake?

"You said this lady is attracted to his type, right?"

"Oh, jeez, that is the understatement of the year. Besides, she's seen him. Believe me, she's eager."

"Good. We'll pick you up at seven."

"All right, dumpling."

Dumpling?

Shannon even heard the smack of their lips as Tom kissed her goodbye. She resolutely kept her eyes on her task so that she didn't glare daggers through Tom as he departed the lab.

She finished filling out the checklist, then carefully placed the slides in their holding rack, and back into the evidence vault. Then she cleaned up her station, slapped off the latex gloves and tossed them in the hazmat bin.

After shedding her lab coat, she marched into Diane's office and waited—tapping her fingers against her crossed forearms while she waited for Diane to get off the phone.

When Diane finally hung up, and swiveled toward her, a guileless smile on her face, Shannon narrowed her eyes. Nothing about Diane was innocent. She stifled the questions and accusations she'd been prepared to hurl at her friend, and instead just said, "Uh, I finished the hair slides on the Keiveken case. If there's nothing else, I'm going to head home. I'm taking Mom out to dinner tonight."

Diane nodded. "Thanks for coming in on your day off."

"No problem."

Shannon turned to go.

"Shannon?"

She swung back. "Hmmm?"

"Where are you going to dinner tonight?"

"I haven't decided. Why?"

"Do yourself a favor, and don't go to Joe Theisman's."

"Why not?" Shannon asked, although of course she knew. The traitor.

Diane waved. "Trust me on this one."

Trust her? Ha! That was a laugh. "Fine." A perverse impulse made her add, "Dumpling."


"I DO NOT want to go out to dinner."

"Tough luck, cowboy," Fletch said. "I'm sick to death of your 'tude, buddy. It definitely needs some adjusting."

Rick glared out the side window of Fletch's car. His freaking partner had all but forced him in at gunpoint. He wasn't in the mood to eat. He wasn't in the mood to make idle chitchat. He was in the mood to hit something. Or someone. Preferably Tom Fletcher.

He rubbed his aching jaw, a by-product of a lucky punch from a two-bit dealer who took exception to Rick's breaking down his front door. "I'm not hungry."

"Fine. You'll be a cheap date." Tom chuckled. "Don't you want to meet my new girlfriend?"

Rick's head whipped around. "Girlfriend? When did you get a girlfriend?"

"See? That just shows how little attention you've been paying lately."

"Who is she?"

"I'll give you a hint. She works at the crime lab."

Rick went still. "Pull over."

"What?"

"Pull over! If you don't want to get us killed, pull over!"

Fletch eased to the shoulder, gravel spitting under the car. Rick threw the car into park, then grabbed Fletch by the lapels of his preppy sports coat and hauled him across the console. "You better tell me, partner, that you are not talking about Shannon."

Unruffled, Fletch said, "I'm not talking about Shannon."

Rick narrowed his eyes for a moment, then shoved his friend back to the driver's side. "Good. I'd hate to have to break in a new partner."

Fletch adjusted his coat and tie, then maneuvered back out into the heavy, early evening traffic.

"Well?" Rick barked.

"Well, what?"

"Who the hell is she?"

"Diane Mackenzie."

"Mack? You're going out with Mack?"

"Why do you sound so surprised? She's a hot babe."

"Exactly. So what the hell would she see in you?"

"Hey! Women love me."

"Mack usually goes for biker types, not prep school rejects."

"Well, she goes for this one," Fletch said, just as he pulled into the restaurant parking lot.

Grudgingly, Rick got out and slammed the door. "I don't want to be here."

Grinning, Fletch met him and slapped him on the back. "Did I mention Diane's bringing a friend along?"

Rick stopped short. "You didn't."

"We did," Fletch averred cheerfully.

Turning on his heel, Rick started back toward Fletch's Range Rover. "Take me home."

Fletch gripped his arm and spun him around. "Come on, buddy. Relax and have some fun."

"I don't want to relax and I sure as hell am not going to have fun."

"How do you know? According to Mack, this woman is hot for you. Apparently she's into grunge," he said, eyeing Rick's attire distastefully.

Rick shrugged off Fletch's grip on his arm. "Who is she?"

"Don't know. But Mack thinks you'll approve."

"Is it . . . Shannon?" Rick asked, hating himself for hoping.

Fletch's eyes flashed with sympathy, which made Rick want to slam a fist in his partner's jaw. "No, it's not Shannon."

Then Rick didn't want to be there. At all. He couldn't imagine even harmlessly flirting with a woman who wasn't Shannon. Which really pissed him off. He hated the weakness, the longing, the wanting. That gnawing need reminded him of his childhood, when he'd fruitlessly wished he had parents who cared, who loved him, who were proud of him.

He wasn't good enough for Shannon. She'd made that

abundantly clear. And still he missed her, couldn't make himself stop loving her.

What a fool.

"Fine," he said, gritting his teeth. "Let's party."

Fletch grinned and slammed a hand into his back again. "Good."

They walked into the restaurant, and headed through the elegant dining area and back to the more casual bar and grill.

Diane and her friend were already there, and when he and Fletch entered, Diane stood and waved, a delighted, almost mischievous smile on her face.

Her friend stood more slowly. He had to admit, the woman was good-looking. Tall and model thin, she had auburn hair and sparkling eyes—eyes he was sure would be green.

Fletch whistled under his breath. "Mack did you proud."

"She's too skinny," Rick said out of the corner of his mouth. But he plastered on a smile as he approached.

Mack's friend didn't even try to hide her appreciation. Apparently she did indeed like the grunge look, considering he wore tattered jeans, a faded red t-shirt and a leather jacket that had seen better decades.

When they reached the table, Fletch planted a big one on Mack, which just amazed Rick. If there were two people more wrong for each other, it was Fletch and Mack. Well, no, it was Rick and Shannon.

"Well, howdy, punkin pie," Mack said to Fletch.

"Hello, baby cakes."

Rick had to keep his jaw from dropping. When had this happened? Had he really been that out of touch with his friends? Another reason to resent Shannon.

Mack turned twinkling brown eyes on Rick. "Cheryl Noff, meet Rick Hardison. Rick, Cheryl."

"Hi, Cheryl."

"Will you marry me?" Cheryl greeted him, in a low, throaty voice.

That startled a laugh out of him. She might not turn him on like Shannon did, but she sure was a helluva lot better for his ego. "Would I have to get a haircut?"

"Oh, absolutely not! Cut that hair and the wedding's off."

Somehow the four of them managed to sit down, Mack and Fletch cuddling across the table, Cheryl uncomfortably close. She wore an emerald green shimmery mini dress that displayed her show girl legs to perfection. Her perfume was nice, but a little too musky for his taste.

They ordered drinks. As he watched Fletch and Mack make goo-goo eyes at each other, Rick resisted the urge to snort. They were laying it on just a little thick.

He took a slug of beer, and almost spit it out when he felt a hand on his thigh. The Coors bottle hit the table with a thud. He turned to stare in amazement at the woman beside him. Why, he didn't have a clue. Women had come on strong to him before and he'd never been startled by it.

She gave him a warm, sultry, thoroughly inviting smile. He tried to return it, but his lips weren't cooperating.

"Mack, can I see you for a moment?" he asked.

"You are seeing me," she responded, fluttering her fingers at him. "I'm right here, silly."

He stood and circled the table, hauling Mack to her feet. "Let's go get another round from the bar."

Before anyone at the table could argue, he dragged Mack to the next room.

"What's wrong, Rick?" Mack asked, frowning in confusion. "Don't you like Cheryl? She seems to like you."

"She sure does. What's she up to?"

"Up to? Why, what did she do?"

"She put her hand on my thigh."

Mack bit down on her lip in a gesture that looked suspiciously like an attempt to keep from laughing. "You're her type. She's attracted to you. What's wrong with her making the first move?"

"She doesn't beat around the bush, does she?"

"When she sees something she likes, she goes after it," Mack said with a little shrug. "She saw you at the police vs. D.A.'s office softball game last spring. When you hit your second home run, she said, 'Who is that gorgeous creature?' At the time you were seeing Lisa Young, and then . . . Shannon." Mack shrugged again. "Once you . . . were free, I figured you two would make a nice couple."

As a cop, Rick had honed his skills at reading body language. Just as surely as every gesture Cheryl had made back at the table signaled—better than a bullhorn—that she was ready, willing and exceedingly able, Mack's body language told him she was up to something. She kept rubbing the back of her hand over her mouth, as if to wipe away a smile. And her eyebrows were raised in innocence, which of course was a dead giveaway, considering Mack didn't have an innocent bone in her body.

"What are you up to?" Rick growled.

"Me?" she said, with a startled hand to her heart—another show-buster.

"Yes, you."

She sighed. "All right, here's the truth." She turned toward the bar and first ordered another round, then swung back. "The truth is, I have a good idea why you and Shannon broke up. It really bothered me. I mean, how can that woman be so silly as to not appreciate you?"

"She appreciates me!" Rick argued. "She just doesn't want to upset her parents." He held out his arms. "I mean, I'm not exactly Fletch."

"Lucky you," he thought he heard Diane mutter. But then she looked up at him. "I just wanted to introduce you to someone who likes you just the way you are."

Rick squashed the desire to boast about just how much Shannon seemed to like him. After all, it would be a lie. Wouldn't it? He studied Diane's sincere frown. Maybe she really had his best interests at heart. "Okay," he said slowly. "I'll accept that."

She grinned. "So, what do you think? Like her?"

Picking up the two wine glasses, he handed them to Diane, then snatched the two sweating beer bottles for Fletch and him. "Well, I don't really know her."

"Since when did you consider that necessary?"

Rick pursed his lips. God, he really was turning into a prude! Well, no way. He wanted his old, care-free self back. With determination, he forced a grin. "True. Lead the way, Cupid."

Her smile faltered for a moment, confusing him. But then it returned, and he followed her back to the table, trying to ignore the dread lumping in his gut.

DIANE WATCHED Rick and Cheryl closely. This wasn't going exactly as she and Fletch had hoped. Rick looked like he was actually enjoying himself. She could see Cheryl was in heaven, even though Cheryl knew all about the scheme to drive Rick back to Shannon. Cheryl was playing the part they'd cooked up to perfection, but Diane knew her well enough to see that her attraction to Rick wasn't feigned.

Leaning into Fletch, Diane pretended to nuzzle his neck. Actually, she didn't really have to pretend because his aftershave smelled wonderful. "I hope this isn't going to backfire on us."

Tom smiled down at her, brushed her hair back, then murmured, "She is awfully touchy-feely."

Batting her eyes at him, she said, through gritted teeth, "Well he's not exactly pushing her hands away, now is he?"

After planting a kiss on her nose, a patronizing gesture if Diane had ever felt one, he said, "Maybe you shouldn't have gotten a drop-dead gorgeous red-head to flirt with him."

Inexplicably, Fletch's admiration of Cheryl irritated Diane. She frowned, until she noticed Rick had turned his attention on them. Pretending to nibble Fletch's ear, she growled, "She's not that good-looking."

Fletch snorted, then covered the sound by coughing. "Yeah, right," he mumbled.

Diane looped her arm through his, then pinched him. Ignoring his muffled curse, she turned and smiled at the couple across the table.

"What do you do?" Rick asked Cheryl.

Cheryl threaded crimson-colored fingernails through Rick's hair. "I'm a hair stylist. And I can tell you, you have great hair."

Fletch snorted. Rick glared. Diane kicked Cheryl under the

table. Cheryl jumped imperceptibly, then turned inquiring eyes on Diane.

Diane smiled sweetly. "You look like you could stand to freshen up. I'll go with you."

Cheryl needed to freshen up about as much as Cindy Crawford needed implants. But Diane didn't wait for her to protest. She stood up and bestowed a loving smile on Tom, even while she ground his foot under her heel. "Be back shortly, lollipop."

"I'll be counting the seconds, buttercup," Tom managed through tight lips.

Cocking her head sharply, Diane signaled for Cheryl to follow her.

They went to the lady's room and fussed with their lipstick, looking at each other in the mirror.

"Don't you think you're coming on a bit strong?" Diane asked.

Snorting, Cheryl said, "Me? I'm not the one calling some guy, who is not even my boyfriend, buttercup, and sweetie-pooh."

"But you are the one who can't keep her hands off the target."

"I thought that was what you wanted."

"Yeah, well, he's not exactly running back to Shannon."

"Maybe he's not as crazy about her as you two seem to think."

"He's crazy about her."

"Too bad."

Diane narrowed her eyes at Cheryl. "Don't fall for him. I didn't ask for your help just to have you come out of this with a broken heart."

Sighing, Cheryl shrugged one shoulder. "Yes, ma'am. So, what do I do now? Back off?"

"No. He'd get suspicious." Diane dropped her lipstick into her purse, then kissed a tissue, all the while her mind working. "What if you give him the big push? What if you make the ultimate pass?"

"What happens if he takes me up on it?"

"True, there is that danger."

"I'd be more than happy to follow through."

"No you don't. He's in love with another woman. It'd only be a rebound fling for him."

"Thanks a bunch."

"You know what I mean. As fun as you may have with him, there's no future in it."

"So, what's the plan?"

Diane tapped her front tooth with a nail. "Hmm, I'm just not sure. Let me confer with my partner in crime."

"BUTTERCUP?" Rick asked blandly, after the women disappeared.

Fletch grinned. "What can I say, I'm overwhelmed with love."

Rick eyed his partner while he sipped his beer. "When did you have time to fall in love?"

"Partner, you've been in the ozone for quite a while recently. You wouldn't have noticed if I'd had a sex change operation." Fletch signaled the waiter for another beer. "So, what do you think of Cheryl?"

"Pretty lady."

"Interested?"

"A man would have to be frozen not to be interested." He saw something flicker over Tom's features but in the dimness of the dining room, he couldn't read what it was. He sighed, then confessed, "I guess I'm still a little frozen at the moment. She seems nice enough, and Lord knows she's beautiful, but I . . . I'm just not in the mood tonight."

Fletch studied his nails. "So, why don't you try to get Shannon back?"

"The stakes are too high."

"Meaning?"

"I suppose if I cleaned up my act and presented a respectable image, she might consider me boyfriend material. But, it just bothers me. It smacks too much of Mary Anne, and how she tried to change me. I am who I am, Fletch. Why can't women accept that?"

Fletch shrugged. "From what Diane tells me, Shannon's under a lot of pressure from her folks to keep their pristine image in the community untarnished. You have to admit, you don't look all too pristine."

"I know," Rick said glumly.

"Does Shannon know about . . . your inheritance?"

"Absolutely not!"

"Oh, come on. You don't think she's a gold-digger, do you?"

"No," he responded slowly. "But, God, Fletch, I got fooled once."

"Bull!" Fletch said, so vehemently, Rick raised his eyebrows. "You knew exactly what Mary Anne wanted from you. She was your grandfather's accountant's daughter, for God's sake. You don't really think she just accidentally happened to be in his office when you had a meeting with him, do you? She wanted your money. You wanted her social acceptance. Bad boy makes good with beautiful debutante. You forgot to consider love because you were too busy being dazzled by her lily-white reputation."

"Since when did you become a shrink?" Rick complained, ignoring the fact that Fletch had just hit a bull's-eye. He'd never loved Mary Anne. Come to think of it, he'd never even pretended to. He'd never once spoken those words to her. He'd just wanted her. Mary Anne, and everything she represented. And she'd been shrewd enough to hold out on him until he'd slipped the ring on her finger.

That damn wanting again. Would he ever learn to control it? And was that why he wanted Shannon so badly? Because she was just out of his reach?

"Anyway," Fletch said, intruding on his morose thoughts. "Cheryl seems to like you just the way you are."

"But, I don't want—" He cut off the thought, and looked down to avoid Fletch's too knowing gaze. Luckily the women emerged from the powder room. Automatically both men stood.

Rick studied Cheryl, wondering why he couldn't manage to drum up a little desire for her. Jeez, before Shannon, he would have happily picked up on her "come and get me" signals and run with them.

Even when he was married, he'd found other women attractive. He'd respected his marriage vows enough not to cheat on Mary Anne, but he'd been tempted. Really tempted. And here he stood, staring at a beautiful, sexy woman, and he couldn't produce an ounce of temptation.

He was in deep, deep trouble.

"Hello, sweet cheeks," Diane said to Fletch, patting one of said cheeks. And not one of the two on his face, either.

Rick rolled his eyes, then smiled at Cheryl as he held out her chair. She returned the smile, though not as seductively as she had earlier. For some reason, Rick felt relief wash over him.

They all sat, then Diane and Fletch immediately started inhaling each other's ears. God, they were disgusting.

Diane came up for air long enough to turn back to them and shoot a strange smile to Cheryl. Almost encouraging.

Rick's suspicions kicked in. He didn't have time to think about it, though, because suddenly Cheryl's hand landed dangerously high on his thigh.

If it had been Shannon's hand, Rick knew his body would react instantly. He closed his eyes and attempted to conjure up some response. His lower half remained disgustingly unaffected.

Cheryl scooted her chair closer, and Rick resisted the urge to back up. Her seductive smile had returned in full force, and then some. Damn.

Fletch and Diane were busy making lovey noises at each other, so he didn't have them to use as a distraction. Cheryl's hand started stroking up and down his thigh, higher, higher.

Rick swallowed a groan, not because she was arousing him, but because he felt bad about his complete lack of interest. He covered her hand to stop the motion.

Cheryl leaned over to him. "How about if we blow this joint?" she whispered in his ear. "Come on over to my place. I'll feed you."

I'll bet, he thought. He wanted to take her up on it, just to prove to himself he could. Unfortunately, he was wildly afraid he couldn't.

*Dammit, Shannon, what have you done to me?*

Shannon, his angel, was the only woman he wanted. That was a fact he might as well face. And Fletch was right. It wasn't Shannon who wanted to see him change. She just didn't want to upset her parents. What was a little hair anyway? What was an earring?

Fletch managed just fine, looking like a GQ model. Sprucing himself up a little wouldn't necessarily be any great loss.

In fact, if a little loss of hair ensured him he'd get Shannon back, it was a compromise well worth making.

Would she take him back? He had no idea. But he certainly wouldn't know by sitting at a bar consorting with a red-head.

Feeling bad, he leaned toward his date. "I'm sorry, Cheryl, really. I think you're a beautiful, beautiful woman. But I'm afraid I'm in . . . involved with someone else."

He geared himself up for an indignant reply or a hurt pout or at the very least a resigned sigh. What he got was a victorious, "Yes!"

Cheryl straightened. "He refused me!" she cried to the two lovebirds across the table. "He refused!"

Diane and Fletch pulled apart, sporting twin smiles of relieved joy. What the hell was going on?

Rick snarled at them. "What the hell is this?"

Fletch jabbed a finger at him. "Face it, buddy, you're a goner. If you could refuse her . . . " he said, cocking his head toward Cheryl, " . . . you're a lost cause."

Understanding seeped in slowly. "You set me up," he accused, allowing his glare to bounce between the two traitors beaming at him.

Diane spared a quick cluck of disgust for Fletch, before turning back to Rick. "Yup," she boasted. "And you swallowed the hook."

"Damn!" he muttered, raking his fingers through his hair.

"You jerks. You're not in love at all!"

"Are you kidding?" Diane scoffed, sniffing. "You don't think I'd be attracted to Mr. Armani, here, do you?"

Fletch sat up straighter, obviously indignant. "Well, who said I'd want to be involved with a . . . with a . . ."

"With a what?" Diane asked ominously.

For the first time since meeting his partner, Rick saw him blush.

"With . . . you!"

"Oh, really?" Diane purred. "You didn't seem to find anything wrong with me this afternoon when you practically performed a tonsillectomy on me with your tongue!"

"That's because you kissed me back! You weren't supposed to get into it like that!"

"I was playing a role."

"Well, me too."

Rick shook his head. They may not know it yet, but Mack and Fletch were in nearly as much trouble as he was.

Cheryl laid her hand on his arm, and Rick forced himself to look at her, embarrassed he'd believed her acting, and had tried to respond.

"I'm sorry," she said softly, with a smile that held not an ounce of seduction. "I hope you're not angry."

He stared at her for a moment, then said, "Well, if you really want to make it up to me, there is something you can do for me."

"What's that?"

"Give me a haircut."

# Chapter Eleven

SHANNON SMILED weakly at her mother as she set the platter of roast beef on the table. Sitting, she automatically threaded her fingers and bowed her head.

Her mother thanked the Lord for the bounty before them and Shannon whispered a hoarse, "Amen."

They lifted their heads in unison, and Shannon began to cut the meat while her mother added noodles and carrots to their plates.

"You still haven't told me why you decided to cook dinner tonight," her mother said softly.

Shannon ducked her head, ashamed that she was too much of a coward to face the possibility, however low the odds, that she'd run into Rick and Diane and Fletch and whomever they'd fixed Rick up with. "I . . . just enjoy cooking for you."

Her mother had been in DC for two days, and in all that time, Shannon had kept up a serene front. But she was close to cracking. She didn't know how long she could stand it.

"Did I tell you that Jamie Culliver bought a huge parcel of land over in Milroy?" her mother asked.

"Yes, yes you did," Shannon said. "That's wonderful."

"Just as soon as he gets his chicken farm up and running, I'm sure he's going to want to settle down and get married. He's always been such a hard worker, just like all the Cullivers. That's a good, solid family."

Except that Jamie Culliver was not much taller than Shannon, and he had a gap between his two front teeth that made him whistle while he talked. "Yes, hard-working is good," Shannon said, because she didn't know what else to say.

Well, she could think of one thing to say. She could say, "I know a man who puts his life on the line on a daily basis, trying to clean up the streets. How's that for hard-working?"

Her mother looked deep in thought. Shannon could just see the wheels turning in her head, searching her list of eligible bachelors. At least she'd stopped condemning Shannon for breaking up with Mark. After a long talk last night, her mother seemed to resign herself to the fact that she wasn't going to have a veterinarian in the family.

"Trevor Whiley finally finished up his master's," her mother informed her. "He's going places. What a smart young man he is."

"Yes." But would he have continued going to school if he didn't have the support of parents? Would he have worked and studied on his own at the age of twelve?

Shannon could barely swallow her own spit, much less food. She didn't think she ever wanted to eat again, if she couldn't share the meal with Rick. Oh, God, she missed him. It had only been two nights, but they were two of the worst nights of her life. Her bed was a mocking symbol of all she'd given up, and she found no rest there.

"Patrick Schindler just purchased a new Quarter Horse. That boy sure loves his horses."

But does he love dogs?

"Charlie Zook—"

"Is about fifty years old!" Shannon interrupted.

Her mother carefully set down her fork. "Shannon, honey, I'm just trying to figure out what you're looking for in a husband. You're not getting any younger yourself, you know."

"Why do I have to be looking for a husband? Maybe I'm not ready to get married."

"You're not?" her mother asked, looking utterly shocked.

Shannon followed suit and set down her fork. "No, that's not true. I do want to get married . . . eventually."

Looking like she might collapse with relief, her mother smiled. "Jonathon Foley—"

"Mother, I'm in love with someone."

Her mother's mouth dropped open. Shannon couldn't believe she'd just blurted it out like that.

Yes, she was in love with Rick. No two ways about it. She was completely, utterly in love with him, and she'd blown it. Because she'd been too afraid to trust her own judgment, to stand on her own two feet and shout to the world that Rick Hardison was the man she wanted, she'd lost him. At that very moment he was out on a date.

Her mother's mouth worked silently for a few minutes, then she finally said, "You are?"

Shannon drew in a deep breath. "Yes."

"Someone from down here?"

"Yes."

"I was afraid of that." Her mother sighed. "All right, tell me about him."

Shannon searched for a way to describe her dream lover. "What would you like to know?"

"Well, the usual things might be nice. What's his name, what does he do, that sort of thing."

"His name is Rick Hardison." She hesitated. "He's a police detective."

"Oh, Shannon, that's so dangerous!"

"Yes, but he's very good at what he does."

"Do you know the divorce rates for police officers? I think it's about the highest, with the exception of actors of course."

Grimacing, Shannon said, "You don't have to worry about me getting a divorce. Rick hasn't asked me to marry him, and I sincerely doubt he ever will."

Her mother looked positively scandalized. But now that it was out in the open, Shannon decided to tell her all of it. "He's my neighbor. We met when his dog broke into my back yard. We started . . . seeing each other." Some things were better left glossed over. Like how much of each other they'd seen over the last two months.

"About six or seven weeks ago, Rick was shot in the shoulder—"

"Oh, my!"

"While he was in the hospital, I took care of his dog. After he got out, well, he was pretty helpless for a few weeks. So I invited him to stay here so I could take care of him."

Her mother's face went splotchy.

Shannon lifted her hands. "I fell in love with him. I tried not to, I really did. But he's the most honorable, gentlest, kindest man."

"Well, if he's so honorable, where is he? Why haven't you introduced us?"

Shannon's gaze dropped to the table and she blinked back tears. "He was still here the night you called. I knew how you'd feel about a man living under my roof. Especially a man like Rick. So I kicked him out."

"What do you mean, 'a man like Rick?' I thought you just told me he's a pillar of virtue."

Covering her mother's hand with her own, Shannon tried to explain. "Mother, he has a . . . colorful background."

"Oh, my!"

"When he was twelve, he lost his parents. For three years, he lived on his own. He was homeless."

Her mother's hand flew to her heart. "Oh, my!"

"But during that time, he continued to go to school. He didn't drop out like most street kids would. He went to school and he worked to support himself."

"Well, that's certainly . . . admirable."

"And instead of getting caught up in that world where he'd lived most of his young life, he rebelled against it. He's now a cop. He hates gangs and drugs with every fiber in him." She allowed herself a dreamy smile. "You should see the way he handles this young man he met. The boy was heading nowhere fast, and Rick straightened him out. He's incredible with kids. He'd . . . make a great father."

"Oh, Shannon, you really are in love with him!"

"Yes, I really am," Shannon said, her heart bursting with the emotion.

"Then why . . . why did you think I wouldn't approve? I can understand why you offered your home to him in a time of crisis."

Shannon's gaze dropped again. "Well, you see, in his line of work he has to . . . go under cover. He has to . . . consort with some pretty bad people. To do that, he has to . . . look like them. I was afraid . . . afraid you'd be appalled."

"How bad does he look?" her mother asked, eyes wide.

"Well, he doesn't look bad! In fact, he's about the most handsome man I've ever met. It's just he looks . . . looks like a . . . thug."

"Oh, my!"

"A very handsome thug," Shannon amended.

"Oh, my!"

Dinner forgotten, mother and daughter stared at each other. Daughter looked away first. "Anyway, it's a moot point, I guess. He was very . . . very angry when I . . . was ashamed . . . " She choked on the word. " . . . to introduce you to him."

"Shannon," her mother said softly.

Shannon looked up. The understanding in her mother's voice stunned her. She opened her mouth, but the doorbell interrupted her.

Shannon's heart leapt. She couldn't imagine anyone who'd come to her home. No one but . . .

Jumping to her feet, she said, "Rick! That must be Rick!"

She nearly ran to the door, stumbling once over a rawhide chew Bert had left behind. Flinging the door open, she had to hide her utter disappointment when her visitor wasn't Rick after all. Instead, Tony stood there, looking embarrassed. Probably because he was holding a bouquet of roses. White roses.

"Tony?"

"These . . . " He thrust the flowers at her. " . . . are for you."

Tony was giving her flowers? "Tony, I . . . don't know what to say. This is very kind of you, but—"

"They ain't from me!" Tony said, looking appalled at the thought. "I told him this was a bogus idea."

"Him?" Her heart started jumping all over again. Swallowing, she said, "Come on in while I get my purse. I'd like you to meet my mother."

Tony looked like he wanted to come in about as much as he wanted to parade through school in a dress, but he reluctantly followed her inside.

"Mother, this is Tony, the young man I was telling you about. You know, the one who's good friends with Rick."

Her mother's eyes twinkled as she greeted the boy. "What pretty flowers!"

"They ain't from me!"

"Well, then, Shannon why don't you open the card to see who they *are* from?"

Pulse racing out of control, Shannon first handed Tony a five dollar bill from her purse, then deliberately pulled out the card and read it.

*White flowers for an angel. My angel.*

It wasn't signed, but it didn't need a signature. "Oh, Rick!"

She whirled to Tony who was busy trying to affect his escape. "Where is he?"

Tony waved toward the front door. "Waitin' out there."

Shannon rushed to her mother, thrust the flowers and card in her hands, then turned and raced for the door. She flung it open and peered out into the night. She saw the silhouette of a man across the street, leaning against an oak tree.

"Rick?" Haltingly, she descended the porch steps. He was the only man out there, but something wasn't right. He didn't look like Rick.

"Yeah, it's me, angel," he said, straightening.

That delicious rumble could belong to no other man on earth. Shannon broke into a run. As she got closer, more details became visible. In the middle of the street, she stopped dead in her tracks.

This was not Rick. Someone was playing a cruel joke on her. This man had short-cropped hair, stylish, but short. Too short. And this man was wearing a suit. Rick didn't wear suits unless he was going to court, and she sincerely doubted any judge was holding court at nine o'clock on a Friday night.

Good thing there was no traffic, because Shannon stood frozen. "Who are you?" she whispered.

He started forward, and his stride sure looked like Rick's. Still, she stumbled backward, frightened of this stranger.

"Shannon, it's me. Don't be afraid."

Definitely Rick's voice. She stopped, and her jaw dropped as he came closer. No one in the world had those coal-burning black eyes. No one but Rick. And that jaw. And that nose. But . . . "My God! What have you done to your hair?" she asked, when he stopped in front of her.

He smiled. Yes, that was definitely Rick's smile. "Got a trim," he said, irony in his tone.

"A trim!" she screeched. "You cut it off! All of that beautiful black hair!"

His smile disappeared. "I . . . thought I'd try and clean up my act a little before meeting your mother."

"A little! You don't even look like you!" She flicked the lapel of his charcoal gray suit. "Where are your holey jeans? Where's your earring? My God, Rick, you look like . . . like Fletch!"

He winced. "Yeah, so? I thought that was what you wanted."

And the realization of what he'd done came crashing down on her. He'd tried to make himself respectable-looking for her mother. For her.

"Oh, Rick!" she cried, throwing her arms around his neck. "Oh, Rick, I love you! Just the way you are. Were. I could care less if your hair is long—in fact, I'm almost certain I prefer it that way—or if you wear casual clothes and an earring." She pushed aside his suit coat and laid a hand over his heart. "It's here that counts, you silly man. You wonderful, crazy, beautiful man. I love what's in here."

"Do you, Shannon? Do you love me?"

"Oh, yes! I've been so miserable. I've missed you so much."

"And I've missed you, angel," he said, his hands gliding up and down her waist and hips, as if in re-acquaintance. "God, how I've missed you."

He kissed her then, a kiss full of promise and love. It was deep and urgent, and bone-melting. By the time he lifted his lips from hers, Shannon was breathless and warm. Very warm. Hot, in fact.

Her eyes fluttered open. She giggled.

"What?" he asked suspiciously.

"I just got done explaining to my mother about your hair and earring and clothing. And now I'm about to introduce her to a Brooks Brothers model."

"You explained? About me?"

She nodded. "I was telling her about the man I'd fallen in love with."

"Shannon," he whispered.

"I was telling her about the man I admire more than any person I've ever met."

"Oh, Shannon," he said, then hugged her to him tightly. "I love you so much."

"I was telling her how proud I am of you, how stupid I was to worry about the outer trappings of a man when there's so much inside to love."

"Shannon?"

"Yes?" she breathed.

"Do you realize we're standing in the middle of your street?"

"Yes."

"And if you keep saying things like that to me, I'm going to make love to you in the middle of the street."

"Sounds good to me."

"And give the neighbors a thrill? I don't think so."

"Darn."

He heaved a breath. "I think it's time to go meet mom."

Shannon giggled at his obvious trepidation. "She'll love you."

He ran a finger under the rim of his collar. "Is my tie straight?"

"You look wonderful."

"I don't have much practice tying ties. Fletch usually does it for me."

"You look perfect." She frowned. "Except for that short hair. We're going to have to do something about that."

Rick released her, and Shannon took his hand and led him

back to her house. That's when they first noticed that Tony still stood there, studiously avoiding looking in their direction.

"Hey, kid," Rick said.

"Yeah?" Tony answered, still not looking at them.

"Here."

Tony finally turned around and Rick dug into his pocket and fished out a twenty, holding it folded between his index and middle fingers. "Thanks."

Swallowing, Tony stared at the money. "Wow. That should put me over the top for that new hoop I've been saving for."

Rick snatched his hand back. "Hold it. If you buy a hoop, you won't be coming around to play ball with me."

"Yes, I will! I'll just use that hoop when you're not around."

Rick narrowed his eyes. "You sure?"

"Yeah."

"Fine." Rick slapped the bill into his palm. "Thanks again, kid. Now scram."

Tony scrammed.

Smiling, Shannon cupped Rick's jaw. "It's a good thing you don't really like that kid."

"Of course, I don't, the punk. Know what he called me when he first saw my hair?"

"What?"

"A dexter."

"A dexter? What's a dexter?"

"I think in our time, we called them nerds."

Shannon laughed and stood on tiptoe to offer her lips. Rick dutifully kissed her, but just a quick peck. He was visibly nervous, and Shannon marveled that anything or anyone could shake up the big lug.

She tugged him into the house, where her mother was now clearing the table of the food they hadn't eaten. At the sound of the door opening, she set down the roast and turned.

Her eyes went round, as did her mouth. "Oh, my!"

Rick hesitated a moment, then stepped forward. "Mrs. Walsh, it's a pleasure to meet you," he said, extending his hand.

Shannon had never seen her mother look like she was about

to faint. Somehow she managed to shake Rick's hand.

"My pleasure. I'm sorry, I don't believe Shannon told me your name."

Shannon choked, until she realized that her mother would never associate this handsome, debonair-looking man with the one she'd just described. "Mother," she sputtered. "This is Rick. The man I was telling you about."

Her mother dragged her gaze from Rick, obviously dazzled by his white-toothed smile. She looked at Shannon. "Hmmmm?"

"It's Rick."

"Rick? Rick? But . . . " She returned her gaze to Rick, whose smile broadened.

"He got a haircut," Shannon explained.

"Oh, my!"

"DO YOU THINK I passed muster?" Rick asked worriedly, as he and Shannon settled on the top step of the back porch. He'd gone to his yard and called to Bert, so Bert now slept on the grass below them.

It was a beautiful night, full of stars and a bright, three-quarter moon. The air seemed scented with the bounty of flowers in Shannon's yard. It was a night for lovers.

"Well, I'd say by the time she picked her jaw up off the floor, she had thoroughly approved."

Rick let out a breath. He picked up Shannon's hands, marveling at her delicate bone structure. She was all woman. And he wanted her to be all his.

"Shannon?"

"Hmmm?"

"I love you."

"I love you, too. Very much."

"You want to hear something funny?"

"Yes."

"I've never told another soul in my life that I loved her."

Shannon went still beside him. "Your wife . . ."

"I didn't love her, Shannon. Not like I love you. I loved

what she represented."

"What was that?"

"Respectability."

"Oh."

"Only I discovered very quickly that respectability does not necessarily breed respect."

"I . . . can't say I'm sorry your marriage didn't work out."

"The only thing I'm sorry about is that I married her at all." He frowned. "Actually, maybe not. I learned something from Mary Anne. I learned that respect has to come from within."

A little sigh escaped her, and Rick turned to look at her. "What?"

She flipped Rick's hand, palm up, and started tracing the lines on it. "I owe you a huge apology."

"You don't owe me anything, Shannon."

Looking up at him, eyes wide, she nodded. "I do. Please let me give it to you."

Uncomfortably, he nodded his consent.

She took a moment, as if gathering her thoughts. "I never gave you the benefit of the doubt. Inside, I knew you were this terrific man, but when push came to shove, I kept seeing you through my parents' eyes. I was more worried about what they thought, how they'd feel seeing you."

"That's understandable."

"No! It's unforgivable." She shook her head. "You know, I think I fell in love with you the first time I saw you interacting with Tony. That's when I realized that there was a heart inside the man. And it scared me to death. I didn't want to know that my lover—my temporary lover—was a very loveable man."

She looked up again, and a single tear fell from each eye. Rick bent and sipped them away, letting his lips linger on her soft skin. "Nothing in the past matters, Shannon. It's the future that matters now."

"Oh, Rick! You're doing a terrible job of letting me apologize."

His lips brushed across her worried brow. "Sorry, angel," he murmured.

That wonderful, maddening little sigh whispered through her lips. "You said you learned about respect from Mary Anne. I learned it from you. There isn't a man on this earth I respect more than you. I love you, Rick. And I'm so, so sorry that I treated you so awfully."

"Apology accepted."

"Why . . . why'd you do this, Rick?" she asked him, running her fingers through his hair.

"Because I respect you, too. I respect your reasons for not wanting to upset your parents. And I'm sorry I over-reacted. Of course you didn't want your mother to come down here and find a strange man—especially one that looked pretty scary—consorting with her daughter. I was stupid to get so angry. I think it was just a by-product of Mary Anne, and how she tried to change everything about me, from the way I looked to the way I dressed to the way I made love."

Shannon stared at him, mute. Finally she found her voice. "The way you made love? Was the woman crazy?"

Rick laughed softly. "No. Just very unimaginative."

She shook her head. After a moment she said, so quietly he almost couldn't hear her. "I'll never try to change anything about you. I love you exactly the way you are. With the exception of that hair," she amended quickly.

"Well, guess what, angel? If you asked for me to shave myself bald, I'd do it. I'd do anything for you."

"Rick," she breathed. "I love you."

He stayed silent for a moment, searching for courage. Finally he dipped into his jacket pocket and pulled out the box. "Shannon?"

"Hmmm?"

"I was going to try and think of a really creative and romantic way to do this, but I guess I'm not very creative, and I certainly am not patient. So . . . here goes." He inhaled, long and slow, then exhaled the same way. Lifting the lid of the small box, he revealed the ring he'd purchased just an hour ago. "Would you consider becoming my wife?"

Shannon's big blue eyes nearly swallowed her face whole.

"Oh, my God."

"I know I can be stubborn sometimes and I know I can be moody, but I also know that I will be miserable unless I'm assured that I have you to come home to every night of my life. I didn't realize, until I came to live with you, what it was like to share my life with someone. Really share it. I want to marry you. I want us to have children. I want to have a family I love and cherish. I swear, I will spend my life cherishing you."

Her shaking fingers touched the four carat stone. Moonlight glinted off of it, making it sparkle.

"My God, Rick! That diamond better not be real. If it is, you have to take it back. You can't afford something like that."

Rick frowned. He didn't exactly want her thinking of his bank balance at a time like this. "Forget the ring. It's your answer I'm waiting for, here."

Her eyes lifted to his, huge and brimming with tears. It was the longest moment of his entire life.

"Yes," she whispered.

"Yes, you'll marry me?" he asked, wanting clarification.

"Yes, I'll marry you." She threw her arms around him. "Yes, yes, yes. Oh, yes. There isn't anything more I want in the world. Oh, Rick, I love you. And, yes, you're stubborn, and occasionally moody—especially when you're in pain I might add—but you are the most remarkable, handsome, wonderful man in the world and I know for a fact you're going to be a remarkable husband and father, too. Oh, yes, absolutely, I'll marry you."

Something roared to life inside Rick. Something almost overwhelming in its intensity. It took him a moment to recognize it as a combustible combination of love and joy. God, if she made him feel this way forever, he was in for a helluva wonderful ride.

Shannon hugged him, alternately laughing and crying, and Rick never wanted to let her go. Thank God she'd said yes. Now that she had, he idly realized how crushed he'd have been if she'd refused him.

Shannon's fingers threaded through his cropped hair. She pulled back and smiled up into his eyes. "Please tell me that ring's a cubic zirconia. I'd hate to start off married life a zillion dollars in debt."

Rick swallowed. "The ring's real. And you wouldn't believe the time I had convincing a jeweler to come down on a Friday night and reopen his store."

He took the ring out and placed it on her finger. It was a little loose, but they could fix that.

"Rick?" she said, staring at it longingly, but sadly. "We can't afford this."

"We can afford it," he replied quietly.

"How?"

His lips quirked up. "We're wealthy, Shannon."

She stared at him. "We're wealthy?" she repeated, as if he'd just spoken in a language she'd never heard before. "As in rich?"

"Filthy rich, I think is how some might describe it."

She looked down at the ring, then back up at him. "You're rich," she said, suddenly making it sound like an accusation.

*"We'll* be rich when you marry me."

She stood up abruptly and descended the rest of the steps.

Rick started to follow her.

She turned around and held up a hand. "No! Stay!"

Bert jumped up and trotted happily over to her. Shannon scruffed his head absently. "Do you want to tell me why you never bothered to inform me of this monumental fact before now?"

"It just never came up?" he ventured, pretty sure she wouldn't swallow that.

She didn't. "Why?"

"Why what?"

"Why didn't you tell me?"

"I don't like to flaunt it?"

"You didn't trust me. You thought I might be after your money."

Shoving his hands in his pants pocket, Rick stared down at his shoes. "Can you really blame me for wanting to be sure you wanted me for me?"

"Did you really think your wealth, or lack thereof, would

have made a bit of difference to me?"

"Obviously not, since you were willing to marry a poor cop." He looked up. "Are you willing to marry a rich cop?"

"Rich or poor doesn't matter, Rick. It's the degree of trust that's in question, here."

"I trust you, Shannon."

"Now you do, since I passed the test."

"No," he said, shaking his head. "It was never a test. I didn't want it to be an issue at all." He shrugged, trying desperately to come up with words that would soothe her, that would put that smiling joy back on her face. "I . . . never asked for the money, Shannon. I was as shocked as anyone when my grandfather left it to me. If you want, I'll give it all away. If you prefer me poor, I'll get poor. Just as fast as I can. I'll do whatever it takes to make you my wife."

She took a stumbling step forward. "Oh, Rick!"

He interpreted that as a good sign and quickly descended the steps. She moved fluidly into his arms.

"Oh, Shannon!" he mimicked, smiling down at the woman he loved like crazy. "If you'll marry me, I promise to do whatever it takes to make you happy. Whatever it takes."

"Do you realize that knowing throwing that annoying little detail in my face makes me respect you that much more? You wanted me to love *you*. I get it. All you have to do is be you. It's the man you are that I love, not what you have or don't have." She smiled that smile that set his heart free. "With one exception."

Alarm rippled up his spine. "What?"

"I'm not marrying you until your hair grows out."

# Epilogue

" . . . MY LAND, Hettie," Shannon heard her Aunt Alice say to her mother. "Using a dog as a ring bearer!"

Shannon suppressed a giggle. She had the feeling Bert was going to be the talk of Belleville for a long time to come.

She looked around the large well-manicured lawn that held tents and tables, some laden with food, most filled with their wedding guests.

It was a beautiful mid-October day, the mountains surrounding them on fire with the reds and rusts and yellows of fall. The sky had never looked bluer, with only a few lazy, puffy clouds ambling across it. The air smelled of roasting meat and roses. White roses. Everywhere. Rick must have wiped out every florist from Belleville to DC to secure that many roses.

Oh, yes, it was a marvelous day. Her wedding day.

"I thought he did a fine job," her mother responded. "And why not? Bert is like their child."

"And he looked so cute in that bow tie collar," Joyce Hostetler piped in.

"And he was so well-behaved," Janice Felbin added. "Better behaved than most children I've seen take part in weddings."

Aunt Alice, obviously not a Belleville native, so therefore not a staunch Rick and Bert fan yet, sniffed. "I was right near the front row, and I distinctly heard the commands they were giving him. He didn't listen to a word they said."

The three Bellevillians exchanged amused glances, but decided not to let poor Aunt Alice in on the joke.

In the month and a half that Shannon and Rick had been in Belleville, Rick had managed to win over an entire town. Of course, when they'd first moved there, Rick's hair had still been way too respectfully short, so he hadn't been immediately condemned as some kind of retro hippie.

As it had begun to grow out, and someone in town would make a point of giving Rick directions to Fred Valley's barber shop, he'd just smile and say, "My future wife won't let me."

Soon the town got used to his hair, and Fred Valley even complained, good-naturedly, that Rick was ruining his business. Apparently a few of the town's young rebels had decided to follow in Rick's footsteps.

Shannon grinned as she thought of the last six weeks. Rick had taken a six month leave of absence from the force because he said he couldn't stand to be away from her that long. They'd moved back to Belleville and planned to stay just long enough for Shannon to complete her commitments to Penn State. Shannon had thought Rick would go stir crazy within a week. Instead, somehow, he'd managed to become the town hero, and most folks refused to admit that he wasn't a native son.

"And that hair, Lettie!" Aunt Alice continued. "His was longer than hers!"

"Yes, isn't it dreamy!" Janice Felbin said, obviously not recognizing the reproval in Aunt Alice's voice.

"Isn't he dreamy?" Joyce Hostetler added.

"Well, yes, he's a handsome boy, all right," Aunt Alice conceded.

"Boy!" Joyce snorted. "That man is no boy. I served lunch at the Smith's barn-raising last Saturday." She leaned closer to her table-mates. "He wasn't wearing a shirt when I arrived." She shook her hand. "Oo-la-la!"

"Is it true you can see the scar where he was shot?" Janice asked in a stage whisper.

"Shot!" Aunt Alice screeched, loud enough to be heard in Huntingdon.

That's when Shannon decided to make her presence known. She moved between her mother and aunt, laying an arm around each. "You ladies aren't gossiping about my husband, are you?"

"Yes," her mother, Joyce and Janice all piped up at once.

Shannon laughed. "Nice subject."

"Very nice," Joyce said, under her breath.

"Are you all enjoying yourselves?"

"Oh, yes," Janice said. "The wedding was beautiful."

"Thank you," Shannon said, smiling goofily. She was so thrilled that Rick had insisted on taping the ceremony. In her totally biased opinion, it was the most romantic wedding she'd ever seen.

When Shannon's father asked Rick, rather ominously, Shannon thought, if he promised to love and cherish her, and all that other stuff, Rick hadn't responded with the standard, "I will." No, not Rick Hardison. He'd answered, "Watch me."

"You are such a jerk!" Shannon heard to her left.

She looked over in time to see Diane and Fletch squaring off. They'd been squabbling with each other the entire week they'd been in town, barely calling off their feud long enough to stand up as maid of honor and best man.

"Excuse me," she said quickly, then moved to intervene.

"All I said was that that color makes your skin look sallow," Fletch said, shrugging eloquently.

The color of the dress was teal, and looked beautiful on Diane. Her long brown hair flowed down her back in shimmering waves.

"Now children, behave," Shannon said, and signaled across the lawn to Rick, who was surrounded by several Belleville natives, all sporting matching awestruck expressions on their faces.

Rick excused himself and strolled toward her, and everything around them melted away. Her husband. He was her husband. To have and to hold for the rest of her life. That knowledge filled her with an almost overpowering joy. She was the luckiest woman on earth, and she knew it.

"Hello, love," he murmured, then brushed a kiss over her lips. "I can't wait till tonight," he whispered in her ear. "I can't wait to make love with my wife."

A thrill skittered up her spine. She couldn't wait either. If it weren't so rude, she'd consider suggesting they cut out right away. They were staying overnight in State College, and flying out the next day to Miami, where they'd meet up with the cruise ship that would be their honeymoon haven.

"I love you," she whispered back, before getting down to business. "But right now I need you to help me referee these two."

"The kids are at it again, are they?"

"They don't even bother coming up for air."

"You are the most insensitive, insufferable, rude, disgusting—" Diane began.

"I love you too, sweetheart," Fletch said, unruffled.

"Ooooh!" Diane growled, then stuck her nose in the air. "I'm getting champagne," she said to the sky in general. "Can I get either of you two anything?"

"I'll take some," Fletch said.

"Get it yourself, bozo," Diane retorted, before turning and flouncing away.

Shannon watched Fletch watch Diane go, and the gleam in his eyes was about equal parts amusement and admiration. It shouldn't be long now, she decided.

"You charmer, you," Rick said. "You have almost accomplished making her swoon into a dead faint."

"I can't help it," Fletch said. "It's just too much fun."

"Leave the poor woman alone, or I'm sending you on pooper scooper duty."

The horror on Fletch's face was comical, and with a mumbled response he quickly walked away. Directly toward Diane.

Shannon and Rick faced each other for a much needed moment alone.

"You are so beautiful," Rick said.

"I bet you say that to all your wives," Shannon murmured, as she tucked his hair behind his ear.

"I'm going to be saying it to this one, every day for the rest of our lives."

"This one will never tire of hearing it."

"Just think, if it wasn't for Bert, we would never have met."

"Bert and his collar."

Rick chuckled. "You were appalled."

"Until I saw his owner. Then I was just dazzled."

"I promise to keep trying to dazzle you for the rest of your life, wife."

"Okay, if you insist. But just remember today, because it's only going to happen once."

He nodded, then kissed her. "Just this once. This very, very special once."

"No condoms tonight, you know. What will be will be."

He grinned. "If you insist."

# About the Author

Trish Jensen has decided that being a romance writer is the greatest job on earth. She gets to entertain handsome men and strong, beautiful women on a daily basis. And she can do it all wearing sweats and no makeup. Her characters know not to complain, because they realize she's learned how to use the delete key.

Trish lives near her alma mater, Penn State, the beautiful, and Amish-filled mountains of central PA with her very spoiled (and Trish still has NO idea how that happened) black lab.

CPSIA information can be obtained
at www.ICGtesting.com
Printed in the USA
LVHW090001190819
628097LV00001B/35/P